EARTH INVASION

Sgt. Wayne Anthony Pope Sr. U.S. Army

EARTH INVASION

Scripture quotations marked NASB are taken from the New American Standard Bible®, Copyright © 1960, 1962, 1963, 1968, 1971, 1972, 1973, 1975, 1977, 1995 by The Lockman Foundation. Used by permission.

iUniverse books may be ordered through booksellers or by contacting:

iUniverse
1663 Liberty Drive
Bloomington, IN 47403
www.iuniverse.com
1-800-Authors (1-800-288-4677)

ISBN: 978-1-4917-6983-6 (sc)
ISBN: 978-1-4917-6984-3 (e)

Library of Congress Control Number: 2015908854

Print information available on the last page.

iUniverse rev. date: 06/19/2015

"Evolution changes within each new birth that enters into this world for we are all one from Beginning to the End."

John.3.15

† *Rest in Peace* Dedication †

God knew you before your Birth…May he know you by his side in the Afterlife for we are all his Children's

My Prayer to All Gods Children's
My…Dad…Jake William Pope…May your Soul R.I.P
My…Mom…Pearl Rose Robinson…May your Soul R.I.P
My…Grand Mother and Father…May your Souls R.I.P
My…Step Dad…Carlee Peeples…May your Soul R.I.P
My…Aunties n Uncles n Cousin's…May your Souls R.I.P
"All my Fallen Soldiers-Family-Friends…Rest In Peace"

Special Dedication
Mrs. George' Annie Kay Richardson
Mrs. Ron 'Linda Faye Adam
Mrs. Charles Yolanda Pope…Lt. Charles. A. Pope…USMC
Ms. Jackie Eileen Pope
Mr. William Jake Pope
Mrs. Carl' Wendy Renae Dixon… Cpl. Carl…USMC
Mrs. Jerry Allen Tamika Davenport…R.I.P Jerry Allen Pope

My Cousin…TERRY BOWEN…RIP

Extra Special Dedication concerning Earth Invasion

Wayne Anthony Pope Jr…Nicholas Cole Pope
Zavion Armad Pope…Jonathan Joshua Pope

My lovely Children's
Prince n Princess
Lacreashia Shantel Pope…U.S. Navy
Wayne Anthony Pope Jr.…U.S. Army
Monique Nicole Pope…Happy Graduation 2015
Nicholas Cole Pope
Zavion Armad Pope
Ayla Amaya Pope
Jonathan Joshua Pope
Grace Tyra Booth Pope

Contents

Novels

Devils Angels Gods Children ...World Wide Seller of a newly earth born species that not just effect man but the entire world. We have no choice but to accept this New Creation or be wipe out by a greater Predator that birth like an uncontrollable disease.

Resurrection an unknown man is born with the power to give life as well as take life, with time is secret is reveal...his ability to change the world before our eyes. You may never sleep the same again in the comfort of your homes nor will your neighbors.

Women Scorned Wendy's Revenge ...when enough is enough and there is nothing left but the hidden demonic bloodline to fight. It take her boyfriend into a world of lust betrayal and never ending terror that get the entire world attention in the worst way. He is left with a lifetime of never ending change in the worst ways known to man.

The Soldier...is a newly Super Hero who dedicate his life to fighting Good and Evil, new creation by man but given immortality from the Creator of all life.

Plantation American is based on a new country within America itself, when the son of a billionaire is publically punished. First African American President must find a way to bring both countries together come or destroy each other.
"Gangster Story"
Soon to be released

"Faith Hope Love." 'Words for the world for we only physically live once."

Chapter 1

"HOMELESS DRIFTER"

Born Date Sept 20 2012

"*H*ey...*get your ass up and get in line like everyone else and if I have to come in there again, it will not be good...so get your black ass up and stand in line like everyone else!"*

His voice was loud as I rolled over looking up at him tasting my own filthy mouth like if I ate a bowl of shit and piss only hours ago.

*"**Now that I have your attention sleepy head...get your ass out of that bed and get to your feet before I come in there and help you."** Correctional Deputy yelled loudly*

I search looking for my shoes, these things was far from that.

*"**Hurry your ass up or do you expect me to stand here and wait for you your majesty?"** Correctional Deputy ask.*

"No!" I responded.

*"**Are you yelling at me you bum?"** Correctional Deputy ask aggressively.*

"No." I responded.

*"**No what!"** Correctional Deputy ask.*

"No sir Correctional Deputy Rinsoen." I responded.

*"**That better and for that little attitude, you are officially on my morning shit list, do you understand me!"** Correctional Deputy Rinsoen ask.*

"Yes sir, Deputy Rinsoen, I understand that im on your daily shit list again as I was before alone with the day before that." I responded.

"Hurry up, there is more than you here son. Correctional Deputy Rinsoen said loudly once again."

It was that moment, my shoes was in the corner as I slip them on before he pulled his baton, this was one of the meanest bastards here. He begun to move my way swing his baton.

"You are really testing me this morning, you think you are special… you are nothing!" 'You are no more importance than boot camp private still sucking on his momma tits son!"

I said nothing, this asshole was looking for someone to strike and it wasn't me this morning that he was going to lay into if I could help it.

"What wrong son, you on don't have nothing smart to say now that im standing before darky right?"

"Deputy Rinsoen, I have nothing to say sir." I responded.

"Move it boy!" Correctional Deputy Rinsoen said mildly.

That moment I started walking but he sent me into the floor instantly without remorse while other Officers stood watching making their commits.

"Say something else son, im waiting smartass!" Correctional Deputy Rinsoen said loudly.

I felt invisible while others inmates begin yelling as they were told to shut the f*uck, this wasn't and ordinary facility. Maybe it wasn't even on the map for all we I knew.

"Get your black ass up or I give you something else to keep you down there!" Correctional Deputy Rinsoen yelled.

I manage to get back up only to be put down again.

"You feel that son?" Correctional Deputy Rinsoen ask softly.

I didn't even respond while holding back the tears that wanted to roll down my face watching him moving in closer like if he was a boot camp instructor looking for weakness. I had no intention of giving him any satisfaction what so ever.

"Hey, this is not the time to be giving me shit…I had a bad night and my wife is on her period again for the second time this month!" 'I can't even eat a healthy p*ssy and if you are wondering why! It is none of any of you f*cking business…now do we have an understanding that

each of you low life maggots do nothing to upset me this early in the morning!" Deputy Rinsoen yelled ever louder.

It was that moment as I was balancing myself when someone said that his wife bleeding crotch must be the best part of her.

"Who in the hell just said that!" Correctional Deputy Rinsoen shouted.

His aggressive movement back and forth walking up and down the line looking at us like some mad man.

*"I will f*ck each and every last one of you up in a matter of second before you can reach back and scratch your filthy smelly ass especially you, late night butt pluggers!" Correctional Deputy Rinsoen yelled.*

No one said nothing as he went back and forth making himself look more stupid than what we already thought.

"Not one of you have a right to call my ugly wife ugly but me, in fact not one of you have any rights once you enter this facility and that give me a right to violate every last one of your once civil rights." Deputy Rinsoen.

No one said nothing, not even when he told us to be a man and take responsibility for our action, this man wanted blood right now. I guess beating up on me wasn't enough for this coward of a man hidden behind a federal badge.

"Every down on the floor!" Correctional Deputy Rinsoen yelled.

This asshole has done some insane shit but this was taking it too far as we all stood looking at him until he started yelling to his Officers to get us down face first. This was about to be a battle as they moved in forcing us to the floor but the majority of us hesitated.

"Get down…get down…get down!"

It was all we heard, there was so many coming our way that it was to many for us to battle even if we wanted to. So much blood was about to this place even for a fight that was far from becoming a riot even if we wanted one with these correctional assholes. Breakfast wasn't a part of me this morning but lunch had been brought as well as dinner. Several days had pass by before we was let out for some sunshine, it was like this from time to time but you had to be tougher than this place at any giving moment.

Often I found myself alone looking at the walls wishing I was beyond them thinking of my days of freedom with nowhere to really call home. Wandering from place to place looking for something that wasn't before me drifting trying to catch what doesn't exist. It was like I was some sort of bottom feeders, relying on myself free from a grounded shelter. Intelligent enough to disappear again once seen but knowledge enough to know of my surrounding for that was my hidden super powers.

I had the ability to be self-educated never relying on the media or what is written in books, my personal experience with a racist society that targeted me upon sight. I embark my adventures upon their eyes that told me how their snow white without out darkness neighborhood operated. Each step I took was unknown freedom but it came without trust as strangers would speak but I loved who I was. Society displayed me as a bum.

Everything I love became my past, abandon like a bag of sh*t as I moved without property or possessions. I had become my own unchanging enemy without commit to anything that I couldn't toss without hesitation. My home was where ever I blended but never flashy enough to be important. No one look upon as important but if so than I was nothing more than a suspicious drifter. I moved about many languages but my politeness only made them glance my way.

My words would be as foreign to them as I was in there land but yet I form relationships snuggling under the midnight skies whenever possible. My hygiene should have been my enemy but it was the opposite becoming my personal moral that allow me roam freely without violence. Positivity and good deeds to others was my strength as well as my cheap travel and bought only what I needed.

"Hey, are you drinking that homemade funny water?" Correctional Deputy yelled through the cell.

I said nothing while taking another sip thinking of my life and the time that I met up with some other drifters before we settle under the night open sky. It had only taking me second to start a fire with my lighter.

"Hey stranger me and the old gal here got some good vittles, you like to have some of this good eating with us?"

Before I could give them an answer, the sound of something rumbling in their bag sounded good.

"I'm ok my friend but I thank you kindly." I responded.

I watched them dig into that stuff like if it was freshly bake meatloaf straight from grandma oven, it was never my thing to eat dog food but there are those out there who craves it.

"Is that garlic you are eating?" Dingy looking woman ask.

"It's good for you miss, want some?" I ask.

"No, doesn't sound tasty at all."

It was ok, we talk about our adventure before I wrapped myself warmly and slept like a baby after a few drinks to quench my thirst. That morning I done my personal hygiene but it wasn't a part of their routine even after I listen to their sexual activity when they assumed I was asleep. Peoples like them was nothing but filth as I made my way away from them hoping I didn't catch anything that they may be carrying between them.

I travel some days none stop on public transportation and clean up during stops while keeping a fresh supply of water. Money itself was never an issue, my service to this country made sure of it monthly plus what I had saved prior. Legal documents kept me from been turned away from been seen as the image of a no account dirty drifter. I wasn't all pure because I have come across an taking things that wasn't mine if I wasn't to be seen but one day I may hit the jack pot and vanished like the wind.

There is nothing like sleeping under the stars but it like the army teaches, when you are not training...you should be sleeping. Sleep is best friends to a drifter and it should be done whenever possible especially when you can do it safely but sometimes a good abandoned buildings can become your savior. Bad weather is our body enemy and it does not discriminate knowing my only fear is being force into slavery. My nationality has had enough of that but when you are far from home, locals know it as well as those who does this for a living.

"Hey, lights out." Correctional Deputies yelled.

There wasn't much for me to do but call it a night and hope for happier painless tomorrow while listening to the guard walking away. It wasn't long after that moment that I had fallen asleep only to wake up screaming, it was like my mind was been invaded.

"What do you want?" I yelled my loudest.

It had taking me a second to realized was it was before calming down, the many lights shining into my cell must to have scared him off.

"What the f*ck is all tha yelling about in here, you ok and why it look like you seen a ghost or some sh*t!" Deputy yelled.

I said nothing as I kept looking toward the corner wall while glancing at them noticing the guard picking up my cup that laid on the floor.

"You been drinking that funny water, haven't you?!" Deputy ask.

I just kept looking around in silence listening to them getting upset'er by the second.

"No more of your sh*t tonight or the next time im going to give you something to cry about…take your ass to sleep!" Correctional Deputy yelled.

He slammed the door told me how pist off he was while listening to his bed buddy say how he hated coming around this room. Sleep wasn't easy as I imagine his frail black frail skin and snow white hair, this darkness wasn't my friend. I tried not looking toward the walls while closing my eyes tightly knowing I wasn't alone. Its energy moving closer and there was nothing I could do while hoping someone return but that wasn't happening.

"What do you want?" I yelled.

I had no choice but to look around while pushing myself deeper into the wall like never before until morning. I had been waking by someone pushing on me.

"Let go…you have to wash your ass before seeing the doctor." Deputy said.

"What doctor?"

"I don't have time to explained to you your entire day, now get your sh*t together and let go now!" Deputy yelled.

I done exactly what he wanted before making my way out as they grab me by my arm while making our way toward the showers. These bastards trusted no one as they stood watching…fags.

"Good morning, it good to see you." Doc said.

I stood there looking at her knowing she knew more about me than myself or at least she thought she did.

"Well' have a seat and let get to this, it shouldn't take long if you answer all my questions." Doc said.

I sat down but the sight of the handcuffs always seem to bother her but not once did she ask them to remove them from me.

"We will be right outside doctor." Deputy said loudly.

"Explain to me how it felt when you first encountered these aliens?" Doc ask.

"Doc, you ask me this before and I always give you the same answer repeatedly. I said.

"Yes you do but I want to hear it again." Doc said.

"Doc, it was hard to believe but I was so drunk off my ass that I didn't know if it was daytime or night but I did notice my food getting lower." I said.

"How did you know that?" Doc ask.

"I don't know but it was vanishing overnight, maybe it was my walks or something." I responded.

It's been an hour and this wasn't going anywhere, she was wasting my time.

"Doc you ask the same question over and over."

Not long after, she called for the Guards, the sound of the heavy doors been open only told me that I was about to be away from this educated b*tch from hell.

"Hey!" 'You enjoy yourself?" Correctional Deputy ask.

"What you ignorant bastards think."

"Watch your mouth inmate!"

I thought about being invaded but I should have known something when I was question about my spending on so much food. Maybe it was my lack of alcohol consumption or the rundown farmhouse.

"Hey, tell me about these aliens." Correctional Deputy ask.

So much anger about this place from cell to cell not to mention there was nothing I had to say to any of these clowns.

"Home sweet home inmate."

I thought about the farmhouse wondering what the hell was I thinking trying to hide aliens that was consuming more food than I could afford. But I done my best knowing they were probably being search for, maybe I should have silence that nosey store cashier.

"You have been buying lots of food and little alcohol lately."

Those were her words knowing several more days passed before I was approached on the yard, these bastards kept me completely isolated from everyone.

"Hey 5051 you are wanted." Correctional Deputy said.

I could see them getting closer.

"You know the routine inmate, don't give us a hard time."

They search me like if I was the deadliest man alive.

"He is clean." 'Let go 5150." Correctional Deputy said politely.

It only taking a moment before the sight of not just the regulars but the military alone with other black suits had come to see me. They introduce themselves and to why they were here, I had been told my entire history. Like if I knew of their existence.

"Could you tell us about your days as a drifter?" Psychologist Terri ask.

"Why would that be important?"

"Can you please answer the question?" Someone else ask loudly with aggression.

"I was nothing no more than just a drifter or as you calls it a bum an outcast to your civilized society."

"Why did you chose this life style when you had your retirement and so much more to look forward to?" Psychologist. Terri ask.

"I needed to walk a little." I responded.

So much written while I listen to how I needed to take this serious for my own good.

"You are all full of sh*t.

"Why did you invest in a farm?" Lady ask.

"I needed somewhere to live." I responded.

I sat in silence.

"Why didn't you alert the proper authority when you discover these aliens, you were known to go back and forth while in the process of running into local law enforcement?" Psychologist Terri ask.

"Where are they now?" I ask.

"That would be classified information on a need to know basis right now." She responded.

"That would be why, the fear of what the government would do to them and if I may ask…how many is alive?" I ask.

"Once again that is classified information on a need to know basis right now." Psychologist responded.

"Is that all you can say?" I ask.

It was that moment I could see all of them written none stop while glancing at me.

"Mr. I see that you are not going to cooperate with none of us and im to inform you that you are to be transferred to a more secure facility other than this place." Psychologist said.

"When and why?" I ask.

"Both questions are on a need to know basis and you will be informed soon." Psychologist responded.

This meeting ended and I was taking back to my cell only to await to see what was going to happen next, this was so frustration. Time continued before I was rudely awaken.

Chapter 2

"Sheriff Department"

It wasn't long after I was awaken by Guards yelling.

"Hey 5150, it time to get that black ass us up convict."

They told me that my ride arrived and that I was to be transferred.

Correctional Deputy Gonzalez? Yelled again.

They wasted no time getting me and my giving crap before escorting me down this long grimly hallway that seem longer than normal this time.

"Hey am im going so early?"

"Shut that sperm in-taker you call a mouth inmate, you will know soon enough!" Correctional Deputy Gonzalez said loudly.

"Asshole." I said lowly.

"You say something guzzler?" Correctional Deputy Gonzalez ask.

"No did you."

Not long after we arrived at some processing area more black suits stood waiting, not one smiled and their silence made them different from these b*tch deputies who talk like little girls. Through them I knew what was beyond these walls, they made sure that it didn't take long process me from this place.

"Are you Deputies serious or what?" Federal Agent Gastellium ask.

"What is the problem Mr. Government Agent" Deputy Smith ask.

"I see razors metal cans of shaving cream and glass objects in this box." Federal Agent Gastellium said.

"What you see is hygiene supplies." Deputy Martinez said mildly.

They were going back and forth but the black suit begin to empting the box completely leaving all razors and glass object behind.

"You can either drink this soda now or we can trash it, which one is it?" Federal Agent Gastellium asked aggressively.

"Can I have my hands uncuffled?" I ask.

He looked at me and then his partner, they both disagreed while moving forward.

"Thanks."

"Hope you enjoyed the soda."

"Agent Gastellium, it was thank you." I responded.

That moment I watch him signed for my released while his partner search me one last time before checking the handcuffs.

"It was nice having you stay with us inmate." Deputy Alcala said.

I listen to him and his friends laugh but I don't think the federal boys found nothing they said or did funny.

Chapter 3

⠶⠶⠶

"FEDERAL DETENTION FACILITY"

⠶⠶⠶

"**D**on't give us no hard time and this will be an easy ride for you, it up to you and you have a long ways to go from here." Federal Agent Gastellium said.

It had taking a while for us to get to where we were going.

"Young man, you to wake up, we are here." Federal Agent Gastellium shouted.

I could do nothing but wake up looking at this man knowing I just left San Diego Sheriff Department that treat me like sh*t and now im in Federal Custody.

"Ok, im getting up."

He even reach inside to help me.

"I'm ok."

He stood back waiting patiently.

"This should be an easy process for you if you allow it." Federal Agent Gastellium explained.

This building scary isolated demeanor wasn't good, maybe it didn't exist on any map and it was like some military style prison. Once we gotten to the door I had look back at the noisy closing gates, this place had so much security. There was so much technology about this place from the coded doors as we gotten inside and they were heavily strapped. I watched them handle my paper work as I counted numerous uniformed guards alone with 3 entry gates.

Once it was all said and done, I was taken to another area before I was search again after the handcuff had been remove. I had been taking to a cell and left for at least several hours before they had return saying their goodbyes. I had been transported again without warning, these boys was odd but maybe this was normal as the first couples of days kept me on my toes. Nothing but question after question it seem, they want to know everything about me.

I didn't say much or even cooperate with them, nothing good was coming of them as they often took me back to my cell. But they came without warning at any giving time.

"On your feet!" Federal Correction Officer Hickly said with aggression in his voice.

I gotten up only to be explained what was to be accepted from me.

"We have to move, so don't give us any trouble."

I couldn't believe that my hand was actually free while walking, this treatment was so different from San Diego treatment.

"You keep acting normal and you can enjoy this little freedom or it could be taken away without notice." Security explained.

But I had a feeling this wasn't going to last even though it made me feel normal.

"This will be your assigned cell for now and im Officer Gilroy."

The sound of an unescapable metal door slam home leaving me alone while looking around the room while holding my bedding and toilet paper. It amazing how big this overpopulated world is until you find yourself in prisoned in a cell that you can barely move. Isolation is not meant for human in this form, this entire process had taken so much from me. Sleep is what I needed but I had awaken getting a reality check of a sink as I splashed my face with cool water before laying back down.

So many buried memories surfaced while looking up toward the ceiling as I gotten back up running in place for a least an half hour before laying back down. My military history was my enemy and without my medication to silence those horrors. They would be awaken with time.

"Hey...wake up!"

I could see someone from my small port window.

"You are that alien guy huh!"

Whomever this was, was nothing more than ignorant as I thought about this isolation alone with how I lived distance from everyone. No one was within 20 miles of me in every direction and now they are all in some form of confinement. So many aliens was facing a new form of living and maybe better than what I had given provided. They were now under government protection but somehow as I could only hope that fear isn't tearing them apart along with betrayal of the worst kind.

Three months came at me like the blowing wind until I had been released only because of our new alien friends…they wanted me to be there. I didn't know what to think when I first heard of this from Mr. Shumuluz. He was their representation attorney that had been assigned to them. What the f*ck is all I could think out loud, this alone is all I could think at first.

Maybe I was wrong for thinking of this once I settle down some. Having my freedom was a blessing as I sat looking at everyone.

"Mr. Baily first the government apologized for the treatment that you have encountered in our system and thank again for the service you have giving this country" Mr. Shumuluz said.

What the f*uck is this monkey sh*t is all I could think while looking at all these black suits that now stood around me. They had so much to say and yet I haven't said a word, not even one.

"Do you have anything you want to say Mr. Baily…he spoke clearly and loudly without hesitation?

"I don't understand any of this, could you explain to me about why am I really here?"

"Ok…Mr. Baily, it like this…what you have discovered is the most amazing thing that has happen to this country and because you haven't really broken any laws." 'You are free to go but our new visitors are requesting you to be there spoke person for them and we can't seem to get them to cooperate with us." 'There is so much we need to know about them and this is your opportunity to serve your country again."

He sat quietly looking at me like if I wanted to be a part of this mess they Have going on knowing that my freedom of roaming and doing what I wanted was pretty much over now. My heart beated faster along with my breathing as I stood looking at him, his body language was telling me that he was getting tired. His bullshit was becoming boring.

"Well! Mr. Baily.

His once calm voiced now displayed aggression and this man wanted an answers.

"Mr. Bergussion?"

"Yes!" He replied.

"I have one question for you, what is my option if I tell all of you to go f*ck yourself." I ask.

His eyes grew wide for a brief moment as I watch him pull out this piece of paper.

"Have a seat and read it!" Mr. Bergussion yelled.

I read thru this none sense.

"This isn't fare nor right."

It was like as if this land of free was treating me like some outcast foreigner or something as I glance at him grinning like if he just f*ck the neighbor cat. This man was truly government trained and nothing more as he handed me an ink pen aggressively.

"Take it!" Mr. Bergussion yelled.

His goons moved closer toward me, this was nothing more than bullsh*t at the highest level and I had to know and hear it from the big horse's mouth.

"This was my life, it not much but it's mines at least and I don't want to be another man in black and I have done my part for the red white and blue...those days are over for me along with the horrors of one to many conflicts."

I didn't want any more horrifying images of lost friends, my battle buddies who no longer walk this earth with me. There never aging live and yet im getting older.

"Mr. Big Ass, sorry sir" I meant Bergussion.

"What now." He shouted.

I just looked at him, his body language was showing aggression now or maybe it was something I said to offend him. I didn't know or maybe it was his overly large plump disgusting big body he had to walk around in for the rest of his life. Or the hidden hemorrhoids from the way he kept scratching his ass secretly like if no one notice.

"Sir, why am I really here and what've I done?"

He just looked at me without words for a brief moment while looking in some awkward direction behind me. Even I had to glance.

"What the f*ck." I said.

Noticing him been hypnotized before asking one of his awaiting dogs if he gotten it out entirely. Laughter came from the others.

"Silence!"

"Are you angry or at least that how it sounded to me?" I ask.

"Sir, he spoke calmly."

"Pvt."

He shouted.

"Have you no respect for yourself?"

"Sir."

He responded in the same tone.

"Have you found it, have you got it?" Mr. Bergussion shouted almost out of breath.

"What Sir?" Pvt. ask.

"The dam buagger…why you keep digging in your nose for." Mr. Bergussion ask.

Once more he responded like if he didn't know what Mr. Big Ass was talking about.

"Soldier get out of your nose, that is disgusting…do you understand me Pvt."

"Yes sir." He shouted.

I could hear others laughing loudly until he told them all to shut the f*uck up…just like that it was silent all over again. I waited for my answer now that the bugger party ended looking at Mr. Big Ass who didn't seem to have much to say or maybe he was choosing his words wisely that exit from his sewer intake.

"Mr. Big but I caught myself about to disrespect him when I noticing him about to raise up from his seat at me it seem but the moment I apologized he calm down.

"Mr. Baily, I personally like nothing about you and frankly I don't give a shit what you do today or the remainder of your worthless bum of a life but I do know that one or two things are going to happen to you in a few minutes." 'You are going to walk through those doors either a free man or in one of my Officers

handcuffs hopefully Pvt. Snot Nose over there." 'Im going to personally watch him handcuff you in the worse way possible." 'That is your choice right now."

He shouted while gasping.

"What so funny?"

"You dying big ass."

There was nothing I could say as I looked at this cheaply printed papers.

"What have I gotten myself into?"

"Stop playing with the dam ink pen."

I just wanted to be left alone the remainder of my life and enjoy what was left of my life while drifting like the wind. So much going on inside my independence knowing Mr. Big Ass hasn't taken his eyes from me not one second. It was like all eyes was on me the second my pen met these document while thinking about how my life would be. Somehow I ended up behind closed doors of until I had been force against the wall, there whispering was so low that I couldn't hear or understand.

This raspy voice entered told me that it was Mr. Big Ass the minute he open his mouth.

"Hey there." I said.

"Mr. Baily, how're you today?" He spoke calmly.

"Im ok, so why did you come to see me…is there a reason?" I ask.

"Well, Mr. Baily." 'I come to see if you are ready to join the team today.

I said nothing.

"You ready to play ball on the winning team or you still being a pain in my ass."

"Well sir, that a big ass you have." I responded.

That moment he moved closer toward me breathing heavily but the moment I attempted to face this lord ass. I had been slammed back into the wall.

"Wow sir, you must really miss me." I shouted.

I could hear him opening up some sort of pouch while breathing heavily but his funky musty sweaty unwashed body was too much to bare right now.

"Mr. Baily, you remind me of someone back in the day…brilliant man but needed another form of persuading to bring out the good that other saw in him."

"Mr. Bergussion would that be you sir?" I ask

That moment I hit the ground instantly when I tried to rush him, I had been almost knocked out feeling pain like never before. He now stood over me looking down smiling while glancing at his soldiers.

"Give him another week to think about the country he love." Mr. Bergussion said.

He walked away breathing heavily while gasping for air while listening to the others following behind him slamming the door. I was alone once more in the darkness with nothing but pain and maybe broken facial bones. Sleep is now what I wanted but that following morning brought another sunrise and there he stood.

"Cheap aftershave, it you."

"Look like you need medical needs their Mr. Bailey."

He wanted to know if I had a change of mind knowing I had no way of winning and with time he knew I would surrender.

"Ok."

"See, Mr. Baily...that wasn't so hard was it son to come to the proper decision that had to be made for the better of this great world that we must all live to learn and share." Mr. Bergussion said.

He look down at me.

"Do what you can for Mr. Bailey here doc."

"I see no broken bones but some major swelling throughout your face." Doc said.

"I know old mam." I said.

"Wow buddy what did you get hit with?"

"Baseball it felt like doc."

"Did they used him you as the glove?" Mr. Bergussion said.

I said nothing looking at Mr. Smelly Ass who continue running his mouth about nothing.

"Doc, I have other business matters to attend this morning, are you going to be ok here with Mr. Baily or should I stay to here giving my support to this matter."

"No doc I have everything under control here."

He looked at doc with this grimly creepy looking smile as I watched him leave after asking two of his soldiers to stand by until Doc leave.

"Mr. Baily enjoy that great decision you just made and im keeping you here a few more days before you leave this great establishment."

"Asshole, what human sperm created your existence."

The sight of everyone leaving told me that I had to stay strong while eating this shity breakfast.

"Enjoy I know you could smell it drifting inside and feel free to scrap the plate."

He had no idea, I ate it all down to nothing but for the next couple of days I had so much time to think about their treatment. But for now I had to keep my mind free but it wasn't until the 4th day when Mr. Smelly Ass stood in my doorway.

"Mr. Baily, you have a big day in front of you."

Those little beaty rat eyes and heavy thicken eyebrows were concentrating on me.

"So are you feeling better and get your ass up, this is your big day buddy."

"Hey…when all hope is lost, there you stand." I blurted out loudly.

I had been escorted from my cell while been told to be respectful but the sight of her wasn't what I wanted to see.

"Good morning Mr. Bailey, this will be short but this is mandatory as I said nothing back, we sat for a few minutes before she really open up her mouth.

"Explain to me how you felt when you were arrested?" Psychologist Terri ask me.

"Who!" I responded.

"Sheriff Department?" Psychologist Terri ask.

"Well … shit happen right." I responded.

"You know we are all friends here right?"

"Hey…you been so smart and all but I know something that you don't, in fact I know peoples like you who master books and taking test aren't even aware of this knowledge." I said.

"And what might that be?" Psychologist Terri ask.

"Now you are wondering what is in my head but you have to say the magic word first." I said.

"And might the magic word be?" Psychologist Terri ask.

"Please, is the magic word…it's please."

"Ok…please."

"I bet that you are not even aware that ghost never hunt unfamiliar areas." I responded.

"Ok and why would that be important and why don't they hunt unfamiliar places?"

"It's because when they dies, their physical life ends and all they know is what they Have known and with that been said, you know now that ghost only hunt what is familiar to them." I responded.

"Ok, now that you have gotten that off your chest, tell me more about how you felt about being arrested."

"It wasn't nothing but a little freedom taking away, wasn't like if I was behind enemy lines or something." I responded.

"Is it because you have experience so much in your military past?" Psychologist Terri ask.

"What're you written a book or something?" I ask.

"Hey…let keep this simple and this is my job is all im doing?" Psychologist Terri explained.

"That morning I had awaken to the sound of flashing lights like if a war was going on but so much, it what I somewhat expected.

I could see him written when I said how this is the Sheriff Department and we have a warrant to search your property…please come out with your hand up.

"Go on." Psychologist said mildly.

"I gotten up looking outside there was nothing good about it, my concern was more for the aliens that I had about the property knowing once they are discovered. All this I had going on was over." "This was nothing more than a nightmare as they lithe this place up and somehow I was no longer a secret." I responded.

"The farm right?" Psychologist Terri ask.

"I invested all I had in this little piece of isolation as I transported them mostly when the sun went down but it was my behavioral pattern that must to have alerted others." I said.

"Why you say that?" Psychologist Terri ask.

"Well, I had started buying more meat than I could even eat possible, it was only a matter of time since I wasn't buying alcohol and cases of beer anymore." "It was only a matter of time before others realized what I was doing *from one week to the next in which turned into several weeks that turned into months." 'So much for freedom and liberty in this land of plenty." I said.*

"Both comes with a price, you should know that more than anyone being a soldier and all." Psychologist Terri ask.

"I do." I responded.

"Tell me how notice your foods vanishing?"

I should have known something when my food supply often had gotten down to nothing, although I was drunk on my ass most of the time. It all happen one day when I found myself in the midst of the night to relieve myself but I can't remember if it was a weekend or weekday. I responded.

"Just do your best, we have all day." Psychologist Terri ask.

"Does it really matter but what I saw was unbelievable and very indescribable even for someone like myself." I said.

"Yes, it does." Psychologist Terri responded quickly.

"First I thought it was the alcohol that I had consumed but as my light search through the darkness knowing deep within myself that I was alone out here and my heart was pounding like crazy while my breathing echoed like bombs in the silence as if a war was going on inside of me." I said.

"Explain the bomb." Psychologist Terri said.

"It was as unreal as I moved throughout the area with fear wanting something to appear knowing I really didn't, the thought alone was making me crazy altogether." I explained.

"Explained how it made you feel crazy?" Psychologist Terri ask.
Silence had come about us.

"Hey, im not crazy and don't you go saying that I am." I yelled.
Silence once more had come between us.

"This is not about you being crazy." Psychologist Terri ask.

"Ok, I see you over there writing a lot, it making me a little itchy over here but whatever it was I had to see what it was…hey does that sound crazy by itself?" I ask.

"No." Psychologist Terri ask.

"Well anyways as I continued breathing heavy with freight but even I knew whatever this must be, it must be afraid of me as well." 'But this strange fear had come over me that somehow I couldn't move another step, maybe it was the intoxication had finally caught up to me in the worse way ever." 'My body needed to sit even if it is just for a minute.

"How long did you sit?" Psychologist Terri ask.

"Im not sure but when I did, my body felt so tired that I must to have doze off and that very moment I felt something run across the top of my head." 'I nearly died when that had happen and when I grab my light to see what it was." 'I was shock at what I saw, it was a child and then it was another one and then another." I responded.

"What the hell" Psychologist Terri ask.

"I know it's hard to believe but I also know that you know that im not crazy because all this is real all and judging by your response just now." 'I said the same to myself but I knew that I had to do my best to catch these things." 'I must to have fallen several times in the process until I knock myself out cold somehow."

"Explained how you knock yourself out cold?" Psychologist Terri ask.

"Well somehow that morning I felt the sun beating on my face as I had awaken with the biggest knot on my head that I was lucky that I didn't split my brains wide open somehow."

"Interesting...can you please continue." Psychologist Terri said.

"Well the next several days of my life was confusing, it was like if it never happen." I said.

"Explain to me what you mean by that." Psychologist Terri said."

"It was hard at first but I had a big lump on my noggin that told me that it was real but it was like whatever it was had vanished in thin air." 'The more time had gone by my darken bruise hurted like hell but deep down I know what I saw and it was my job to find these things." 'My alcohol consumption was getting lower and lower the more I search and me not making it to towns to buy more had made it even worse." I responded.

"How could you find anything being drunk on your ass?"

"That not a professional tone of voice." I said lowly.

"It wasn't easy but I fought many conflicts and with all that behind me I knew it wasn't going to be easy but what is in life." 'With all the experience I had under my belt, nothing I done for my country even compared to the devastation and destruction that I have seen."

"Did you know some of the aliens retaliated with death?" Psychologist ask.

"Yea, I do." I responded.

"How does that make you feel?" Psychologist ask.

"Now you explained to me what the hell you mean by that Mr. Know It all?" I said loudly.

"Calm down it was only a question but I see you are taking it to the heart with much aggression." Psychologist Terri ask.

"Whatever!" I responded.

"What I meant was how you felt about them killing several cops and emergency staff not to mention the civilians until they were all caught."

"Ok, how would you feel if your family was attack without notice and murder?" I ask loudly.

"Calm down but you are on the track, now explained to me how you felt overall?" Psychologist Terri ask.

"How did you expect me to feel but so much happen so quickly that even I was surprise but I expected it to happen in so many ways." 'All those flashing lights and eventually Helicopters coming from a distance but when I heard gunshots I knew it was over." I said.

"Keep talking, this is what I need to hear."

"I fought in many conflicts for the love of so call liberty and freedom and took many lives before I even knew it and I guess the police acted just how I would have." 'Not one of them expected to come in contact with an Alien Species that had the capability of taking their lives as well." I explained.

"Now about the civilians, how did that make you feel?" Psychologist Terri ask.

"I had no control of that but I don't blame the peoples for wanting to destroy the unknown, I guess I would have done the same and I heard gun sale sky rocketed overnight...was that true?" I ask.

"It was true and many peoples died from their attacks, it had gotten so bad that the National Guard had been activated." Psychologist ask.

"Well at least it's over with now."

Chapter 4

⌘

"THE SIGNAL"

⌘

"They have now been with us more than 10 years now in complete isolation and many believe it was the worst thing ever. Many countries have come to America to study these many Alien Species that has strengthen our technology. We learn so much about them and although they presented no fear, it what they represented. Maybe if we didn't give them the best possible living conditions hoping they don't become our destroyers someday.

But we monitored them like a new born babies knowing they were kept from technology and for bidden to manufacture their own. But even I knew there was only a matter of time before something happen involving them and technology. Everyone known from the way they learned our languages that their knowledge was beyond ours. And with time a signal was sent beyond earth and this was the beginning of an entirely new beginning.

We all knew that change was destined to come from it and somehow Harvard Space Department had intercepted the response and from the rumors I heard…NASA and Government was alerted. Not really not sure who was alerted first but I guess it don't matter. It was rumored that the President first words was wow…funny huh?" There should have been a greater response but maybe I would have said the same if I was in her shoes. But how could you not expect something like this to happen knowing too much time pass by without one incident.

So much information had been gather about what we only thought existed causing us to become relax. We actually allowed aliens to work directly with the smartest minds that existed among us. Dr. Jerry Ahtmans designed this new telescope in Tucson Space Center in Az. His studies of earth gravitation rotation field discovered this strong signal claiming that it speed was unbelievable. Many countries gotten knowledge of this and felt that America was holding back alone with new technology.

They feared that it would be use for spying on satellites radar systems. Some feared this could bring us to the brink bringing war upon our militaries or even Def-Con 4. This new vision telescope was fixed mounted but the technology that had been created by the aliens made it equal to sound waves. Nothing like it has ever been seen because it could be operated like a home station and transported like radio waves upon aircrafts to battleships to the smallest vehicle.

America had the edge over the world making them more dangerous than they already was, with these new Aliens in our care. We had the biggest stick and many Foreign Countries wanted this technology as well, it was only a matter of time before they acquired it as well…by any means necessary. I never knew why I was always around, maybe it was because I was the first to encounter them and it was me that they trusted. But it wasn't all gravy and hot butter biscuits straight from the over, many had died in the hands of ruthless soldiers who feared them and mad scientist who dissected them like frogs or something.

I witness the goodness of this country but I also saw the horrors of what we had done to get such information that better our lives. Medical Teams from all around the world made discoveries that would have never happen if they didn't make their way to our world. If I saw my family mutilated before my face, I wouldn't just have a chip on my shoulder of revenge but something more devastation that even I would not believe once it happen. It was determined that the signal that was sent was so fascinating that it travel beyond many solar systems making it undetectable.

This technology that we had been giving had hidden codes that we never even had knowledge of alone with it gradual increase and decrease. They had taking what we known as computer virus and giving them life within our own system intensity, these extraterrestrial recurrence signal would become invisible to our detection array. Once it was discovered it had become a task to find who had been sending information back, this country felt threaten and after searching but coming up with no answers.

A special unit had been giving the task of getting the information needed, it often resulted in brutality and numerous deaths of the Alien Species but 10 years of living without the fear of being murdered or hunted had cause them to multiply.

These species develop a good size population and the one that was found to be of no threat had become members of our society. I hate to say it but some even replace the normal house hold pets like dog and cats. As much as they were monitored, they reproduce and was sold on the black market and even with the harsh penalties that had been set forth by laws. Many still took their chance on owning what was highly illegal, it was the spread of diseases that gotten many citizens caught and airborne pathogens that would bring on forms of incurable sickness by man medicine.

This was the main reason why anyone that had one in their custody had a special government license. Not to mention that there was a special agency that monitored them without notice. I myself thought it was a great idea as I gotten to know some of them personnel and they were as helpless as a baby lamb. But there were others with explosive aggressive tendencies and deadly behavioral pattern that needed to be kept in confinement under watchful eyes to the best of our ability.

"We now know that Extra-Terrestrial exist among us now as we have them here with us and several walking around the White House, but these strange radio waves distance from us is unknown." President Hillary said.

Silence had come about for a brief moment.

"How do we know if they aren't Russian or some other higher tech country with some advance satellite system that we know nothing about?" President Hillary ask.

"We contacted the Russians alone with others countries that has that capability and they have all responded that it is not there's." NASA Advisor Mr. Garland responded.

"It belong to someone, it has to someone other than ours and I want answers." President Hillary blurted loudly.

"Madam President, if we receive radio contact, even 10 years ago, it would take another ten years for them to even make physical contact with us." NASA Advisor Mr. Garland Responded.

It was that moment she just looked at him and laugh, we wondered what was so funny as we had done nothing but look on.

"Were in the hail do you guys come up with these calculations, whatever is out there isn't going to be here in 10 years, more like 10 days for all we know." 'I want some answers, so no matter what you have to do to get my answers." 'I want them now!" President Hillary shouted.

"Madam President, this is communication from Australian astrologist pick up voice patterns before it was scramble somehow by their technology from us." NASA Advisor explained.

We sat listen to this language that we never heard before as he explained how it been cross with every documented language on our planet.

"Madam President, there is a similar language spoken on this planet." NASA Advisor Mr. Garland said.

"Ok, where is this mystery language?" President said.

"Africa, but the tribe lives in isolation and pose no harm to us or anyone." NASA Advisor Mr. Garland explained.

"Ok, what did they say?" President ask.

"Madam President, their words was concerning about their engines and a new solar system they were entering." NASA Advisor Mr. Garland explained.

"Thank you, now we know that the realization and proof that we are not alone in this gigantic universe and that it is causing an intense impact on our scientific perception intelligence." 'If…aliens do make their presence, we must remain calm and even more professional." President Hillary said."

"Madam President, the Royal Humanity of London offers unknown source of extraterrestrial information of radar signal broadcast having evidence of intelligence within their life form." 'Many peoples laugh at them but since we have Alien Life, they are highly valuable for what they can offer." NASA Advisor Mr. Garland explained.

"So, what're you saying directly?" President Hillary ask.

"Well, we have been working with them now for over 10 years now and it would be an honor for them to sit and give you more professional information on this subject Madam President." NASA Advisor Mr. Garland explained.

"Madam President, if I may add, the problem with us is that as technology expands, we are making ourselves more and more efficient, meaning that we are making our signals fainter and fainter," NASA Advisor Mr. Garland explained.

"We transmit signals with everything we do from cellure to our own operational satellites of billions of megawatts and im sure they can be picked up relatively easy across the depth of space."

Silence had come about us but I could tell by the look in this arrogant son of a cocky b*tch wasn't going to let her opinion be that last of it as he sat twiddling his thumb in frustration of being told less.

"Madam President, all that im saying is that with technology, as we switch from analogue to digital broadcasting we will become four times fainter because digital uses less power."

"So you say we will eventually become undetectable?" President Hillary ask.

"Yes." He responded.

"So, what is true for man, maybe true for Aliens?" President Hillary stated.

"Some of your smartest scientist are working with the Royal Society and it Astronomers, you known they Have detected planets no bigger than earth orbiting stars having continents and oceans." NASA Advisor Mr. Garland explained.

"Really, have you personally verified this information?" "Not exactly, but if they say it's true…im sure it is." NASA Advisor said loudly.

"One question, don't you have financial shares with them, it what im told and are you trying to sell me into something?" President Hillary ask.

"Madam President, im just here giving you our latest information and letting you know that they will be more than happy to speak with you in person on their latest research, Madam President."

With that been said, im sure that this meeting was coming to an end, this lady has a short tolerance for gold diggers of any kind. We watched her move about us in silence like if she was waiting for us to say something but no one did.

"You been mighty quiet, to quiet for me and to let you know, I like the wildness in you as your words comes with a sense of reality." 'What is your opinion this meeting?" President Hillary ask.

"Madam President, extraterrestrial information would benefit all of us right now, photos of other unknown planets is beyond us just like we are beyond monkeys ruling our world." I responded.

"Ok, I see you are very deep today." President Hillary said.

Maybe, I should have just stayed quiet and, my breathing had become so heavy thinking how it not long ago, my life was like a nightmare. My life had change from the hands of another and with time it brought my drinking to almost none existence. But I face another demon as the spotlight had come into my life, even now this presidential shadow has placed me into a life that I have avoided since my days of military service. It wasn't long after as I ended up back home relaxing.

Chapter 5

"World Disruption"

Our satellite pick up this unknown signal of nearly 3 miles wide and many smaller ones moving past Jupiter on their way toward earth. It was our space shuttle that confirmed it just before their disappearance. It wasn't long after that we begin to feel this strange disruption among us, it brought nothing but fear to our daily lives and yet there wasn't anything that could be done. I knew the real story but the media itself could do nothing but believe the lies that they were being told.

They were under presidential orders but even I knew that a lie was better than the truth right especially right now. We are nothing more than human and it doesn't take much to send us into panic mode making us even crazier and that alone make us dangerous. And yet they call animals wild but yet we will destroy each other in the blink of an eye without hesitation. What we were facing was a unique moment in our history, this could be a rapid age of social and planetary change.

The world has known for years that we are not alone anymore as I could remember from day one of our reaction when the President first inform America. The way peoples reacted shouldn't have been a surprise to any of us as the store emptied out and peoples pulled their saving from banks not just here but around the world. So much had happen to us before they made themselves known and I believe that we wasn't the first to even feel the impact as we had even experience a change in atmosphere. The media kept everyone at ease by mention that we were experiencing a rare climate change that happen every so many thousands of years but I knew better for some strange reason that it was nothing more than another lie.

Our balance of life had be disrupted. The food supply was even been effected, this alone sent us into some form of panic we produce was been sky rocketed as our own government tried to undermine the nation itself around the world. Our own food banks had slipped up themselves by releasing critical information of our rising population as everyone has a high demand for meat. We were facing some sort of nutrition shortage for the world poor alone with increased greenhouse gas emission from livestock especially in developing nations. We were heading down a dangerous path of rising hunger for meat within the upcoming years if this climate continues on it path of destruction.

Panic made its way into our homes when the one country that no one gave a shit about us been affected. Africa was been blame for 30% of global warming greenhouse gas emission that it livestock which typically graze on marginal land and crops residue had become greater than that of a hundred times over than develop nations trajectories. Peoples panic when they discover what a few degrees in temperature could do to the world food supply, even the river deltas of Asia. It provided two-thirds of the world rice had become vulnerable to the rising sea level from the many unpredictable storms that appeared like an avenging ghost according the China Daily.

Ugandan farmers who grew bananas and coffee felt the change with less productivity of crops from land erosion due to massive flooding. America done their best to provide for the loss around the world assisting the World Bank of United Governments. Our climate was being threating by an Alien Foreign Objects floating above our outer space moving at remarkable speeds. It had become a major topic among or world, we found ourselves being blame by the Russians China, even our allies like Germany and the Brits along with many other Europeans countries.

It didn't take long before they realized that this unknown technology designed wasn't ours and begin to blame each other. This had become nothing but fuel for New Reporters that only brought freight upon our existence. It was to my belief that we were being tested on our reaction to see how fast our so call civilized peaceful society can turned on each other within the blink of an eye. So many wars have been fought among the nations of the world but somehow this unknown force. We had no control over, this was only bringing havoc upon us, it seem like it was an impossible fix.

It didn't take long before the power houses of the world tried to put their past behind them and come together. Our own enemies seem to be within ourselves as every country was releasing information concerning the world meeting while basically blaming each other. This alone only sent its citizens protesting and rioting while blaming each other for the effects that disrupted their daily lives or the comforts of their own countries. This foreign global warming was destroying food production from the biggest countries to the smallest.

Who was now coming to life accelerating sever pervasive and irreversible international economic disruption impact. China who stated that this alone could be a technical ingredient start up for advancing technology companies to grow. But there isn't any or at least not in a conventional sense yet, we are on the verge of destroying ourselves over what hasn't been proven or even displayed hostility. We knew that we wasn't alone once reality had been displayed before us over ten years ago.

Iteration an intellectual had distinguished us from any other existing species bringing investors worldwide to be a part of our great discovery. That following day I had been ask to attend the White House meeting as I sat around the round table once again.

"Mr. Mc Hunz, you have a doctoring in Alien Science, could you please inform me what we were dealing with alone with the outcome we face?"

"Yes, Madam President, in my years of study alone with world travel, it is my experience that if aliens came to us as more than friends and they became hostile in anyway shape or form." 'It would not be a good outcome but as im sure you have sent team of photographers and professionals."

"I did." President Hillary responded.

"What im saying is that who would not want to capture such an event, but this can be a tricky filming an Alien Invasion would put that person in the overnight spotlight in the middle of the first attack wave." 'But that person should be careful not to take filming duties too seriously."

"Why is that Dr. Mc Hunz?" President Hillary ask.

"Well, it not reality for mere survival, like if Holly Wood movies that faces it characters are face with gigantic extraterrestrial creature striding before

them is ridiculous as they never put cameras down in the face of death." 'It not reality because fear alone want alone such unreal bravery behavior." Dr. Mc Hunz replied.

"What if they are subtle to invasion?" *Secretary of Defense Allison* **ask. "What happen if they are not subtle and they enter our planet via seemingly innocuous meteorites, and they become aggressive spaceship with a disastrous and reap havoc upon us"** *Dr. Mc Hunz said.*

"NASA has evidence of alien life." General Talley shouted.

"Really, where?" *I ask.*

"Do they have enormous green eyes and they wore no cloths?" Dr. Mc Hunz ask.

It had gotten quiet as no one said nothing in response.

"Peoples, despite their technological superiority, it's possible that aliens may have an interest in our planet but if we become aggressive." 'We may initiate a war." Dr. Mc Hunz explained.

"So you are saying for us to do nothing?" President said.

"Im asking you to elaborate first if we are invaded and keep in mind that what normal to humanity maybe toxic to them." *Dr. Mc Hunz said.*

"Alien comes in many predominant forms according to abductees testimonial and somehow we seem to be defenseless and less complex organism, but you saying if I sneeze on them." 'It could destroy them?" Secretary of Defense Allison ask.

"Exactly but the same as we have that power, so do they as we are not immune to the disease and bacteria's that they may inflict us with as well as leave behind and hope not that our females are capable of bearing their kids if that should happen." *Dr. Mc Hunz said grinning.*

Sick bastard is all I could think when I saw his wicked sicken smile as we all gotten quiet for a brief second.

"We are getting far from the subject at hand here Dr." *President said.*

"What're you asking me Madam President?" Dr. Mc Hunz ask.

"You are the subject matter of extraterrestrial visitation, I need to know what could happen to us as a whole if an invasion takes place" *President Hillary ask.*

That moment he push back in his chair before getting up walking toward his Staff who was setting up the film monitor.

"This is going to take a moment while she set this up, it will help you all to see what may happen if an aggressive invasion should happen." 'But let me speak a little on the topic first." Dr. Mc Hunz said loudly.

He move about like a professor without fear in his classroom among the most powerful peoples of our time.

"There is always a countdown from the beginning that we have no access to it timing or how it will come about and happen." 'This extra-terrestrial intelligence and all we can hope is that they come in peace." Dr. Mc Hunz said.

"What if they are hostile" General Talley ask.

"We hope not but if there visitation is hostile, it may be surprising in the worst way." Dr. Mc Hunz replied.

"Im more concern about our world, especially of our economic." President ask.

"Business should go as normal Madam President but with time if nothing is done and people begin to fear the unknown that it may bring." 'Peoples will be fascinated at first from sighting that will produce more sky watchers, even more so with our overnight technology and web cams." Dr. Mc Hunz said.

"I want to know about the contact?" President Hillary ask somewhat loudly.

"Madam President, many astronomers will race to analyze their coming, their great distance above our earth. '10.000 kilometers, maybe more...closer than our own moon." 'Their creeping near earth without warning will bring more and more fear among us." Dr Mc Hunz spoke with confidence.

"Our satellites that will track there every movement as they move closer to us." Admiral Thornton responded.

"Our military will take an anomaly once U.S. Space Command gets involve with it global satellite tracking systems and high power telescope and radar will search for any unknown airborne that may be a threat to us." Air Force General Keaton explained.

"U.S. Space Command alone with its astronomers looking on will give confirmation that it's a real UFO and not just space garbage finding its way

into our solar system and that it is power by some source of energy." Secretary of Defense Allison responded.

"United Nation Department of Outer Space Affair Committee will try to transmit a simple message to the UFO with radio signal waves simultaneously in most worldly spoken language like English, Spanish, German, Russian, Arabic, Chinese and even Hindi hoping to get a response." NASA Director Furor spoke.

"And if they get no response than what" President Hillary ask.

"We will than respond with universal language of mathematic in a sequence of prime numbers." NASA Director Furor replied.

Amazing having all these Albert Einstein's putting in their 2 cents, it would be nice if they all just shut the f*ck up and let this man talk for a minute.

"You have been so quiet, what your opinion Mr. Baily?" President Hillary ask.

*"Madam President, we are a decision away from Armageddon, I may not have a college degree or doctoring in education but I been a soldier and fought and seen more death than I care to remember." 'America has put more money in me than probably anyone who sit here." 'Therefore if we are invaded, this economy will go to sh*ts within time, if there is an invasion upon us, we must come together as a whole to defeat whomever is coming." 'We can't have enemies within our own world, unification and one centralized authority of mankind's is our only faith if this planet is attack by an Alien Force without provocation." 'We must become one world government Madam President." I said.*

"Ok, very well spoken, much more than I expected." President Hillary replied.

"What he speak is true but before all that we must explore the possibility of an Alien Invasion, many Presidents of the past like Bill Clinton spoke of aliens and how he feel that we are not alone and that we may become divided as a nation." Dr. Mc Hunz said.

"If I may Madam President, I always felt that we are not alone in this universe as we now know that we are not." 'If they come hostile, I see a great war coming our way, not just from the Extra-terrestrial but globally from other nations of this war from fear perhaps." I said.

"Explain more about your meaning of fear perhaps. As I don't understanding your meaning." President Hillary said.

"America back down from no one and if there is something that put them in fear from us and we don't give in." "The only way to calm down a neighborhood bully is to come together as one to defeat him and not by yourself or nothing will get down." I said.

"So we are that bully?" President Hillary ask.

"Yes, Madam President, we are." I responded.

"Ok, maybe you should have my job." Secretary of Defense Allison responded from thin air.

"Maybe he should." President Hillary responded.

Silence had come about us for a brief moment.

"Madam President, We have develop a space base weapon system designed to Penetrate Alien Invaders before they get to earth atmosphere, it highly classified and very capable of destroying anything within it range as they orbits earth disguise like satellites." NASA Director Furor said.

"What weapon?" General alone with the Secretary of Defense Allison responded at the same time loudly.

This was new, not even the President was aware of as she told the Director how she wanted to know more of this unknown weapon.

"Weapons are not the answer here Madam President and if we fire upon what we know nothing about, we could trigger a war that we have no chance of winning with our primitive weapon systems." Dr. Mc Hunz replied.

"It clearly that there is more intelligence life out there that may be hostile to our environment and we will do all we can to keep the peace while protecting our resources but we will die before we are colonize by anyone." This meeting is adjourned but I want you will to be on standby if need and no less than an hour from the White House including you Dr. Mc Hunz, im sure your expertise will be required. President said.

That was the best news that I had heard as I found my way heading home.

Chapter 6

"First Encounter"

NASA Board on Extraterrestrials confirm that alien invading earth may be within our near future from outer space. It wasn't long after those exact words something appeared like a storm of ghosts from the darkness of clouds sitting high above Seattle Washington airspace. It caused everyone to fear the unknown as it took us several hours to get there from our location. I saw this with my own eyes with such disbelief that it was even hard for me to accept.

I stood thinking about what the other billions now thought from their homes and portable technology. It was like looking into two worlds now becoming one feeling this old woman who I never seen before grab my hand. It could've been nothing but fear that she was experiencing.

"Who are they and why is they here?" Old woman ask.

I had no answer while feeling her squeezing my hand like a mother giving birth.

"Is that smoke I smell?" Old woman ask softly.

I was without words once again while looking at this phenomenon that even I couldn't explained if my life depended upon it.

"I hope they are friendly." I responded moment later.

My word was not comforting as we both stood looking at these darken clouds burn red hot surrounding this Unknowns Alien Entity. I remember only months ago when we first discover this and we told the public nothing but lies to keep the peace. There was no way of hiding this if the world depended on it as we stood watching. It was that moment something had begun to appear breaking thru the burning smoke as panic and kayos formed around us.

We knew that we was no longer along when we taking on these alien's from another world a generation ago. I never thought that something like this could happen as it displayed itself before us.

"Is that a spaceship?" Old woman ask.

For the first time I responded instantly while listening to those around me going crazy.

"Get back was all I heard." It was my own Command.

That moment I felt the old woman grab my hand even tighter while pulling away from her.

"God will protect us." Old woman said.

I felt her pulling me even harder while nothing but panic was going on. Nothing but accidents and panic was going on causing many accidents while sirens could be heard in the distance coming our way. I kept moving toward my awaiting helicopters as we could see this massive things been more than a mile in length.

"Do not fire!"

It was all we could hear was the General in charge yelling, even if someone did...how much damage could they actually inflict upon this technology that we knew nothing about. Once we gotten off the ground, we hovered over the city along with others that look on from a distance. I wondered if we were safer on the ground as more units were arriving from all directions of the city. The alien moved closer toward hovering high above us all.

"Return back home." Base Command instructed.

We have officially being invaded as we could see another one breaking thru the clouds while so much communication was going on around me.

"This once quiet city was destined to become a battle zone by the end of this very day." I said.

We could see medical sirens fighting thru scattered traffic knowing this was nothing but the beginning. Nothing long after we had return to base seeing another one break thru.

"This was far from the stone age." I said loudly.

It didn't take long before NASA confirm our alien invasion of these massive spaceships but the media took it a step farther. They spoke of a continuing invasion from numerous top reporters, it was nothing but ignorance. We should have been working together avoiding major panic knowing nothing was going to cover up this invasion.

"We can avoid a war." Homeless man spoke out loudly to the media in Texas.

Many scientists spent a lifetime searching for extraterrestrial intelligence had been giving there answer over 10 years ago. I sat watching my television the best I could because numerous stations was fading in and out.

"Im…Dr. Likos of New Mexico Space Center, these invaders are none aggressive and they are the same as what we have had for nearly 10 years with us."

He spoke to the media but what did he truly know of their intentions or if they are different of what we have in our custody. That early morning I had awaken to the news as I begin eating.

"This invader could be a scout before the following Army is to come in increasing numbers to our planets." "This alone is the best reason of why we are effected with rising greenhouse climate emission as they must've some system that can change our atmosphere drastically from afar while posing a serious threat." Dr. Livingston said.

I didn't know too much about what he was talking about but it didn't take a rocket scientist to figure out that if this was possible. Our symptomatic technology nor our ability was no match for there's as I listen to another scientist days later from the U.N. Panel of Extraterrestrials confirm to the world that we are being invaded.

"It's been predicted that humanity will've direct encounter with aliens and we have collected plausible conclusions." Dr. Livingston said.

He stated the consequence of a close encounter that would help humans prepare for this unknown moment that this could be neutral encounters.

"This could be less rewarding because humans maybe be indifferent towards aliens but it may also be beneficial and peaceful in which extraterrestrial intelligence." Dr. Livingston said.

What I experience within the last ten years of our extra-terrestrial encounter has giving us insight on new technology from their sickness to curing diseases that killed us with time.

"There may be a harmful outcome that the alien may attack and enslave or maybe even use us as a source of food upon their arrival."

I could only imagine what this world was thinking when they heard of the possibility of annihilation of our civilization. Hoping they don't unleashed hostile artificial intelligence or perform catastrophic experiment.

"Even though extraterrestrial has been discovered, there is still much needed work to be done and the age old question." 'Are we alone in this universe or is there other intelligence other than us couldn't be answered with our Hubble Space Telescope has giving us so many surprising things." 'What has come to us defines the knowledge of planets having atmospheres similar or equal to ours." Dr. Livingston said.

It wasn't long after the President call a meeting of world leaders and now I can see why I never wanted a life of politics. This seem to be nothing more than headaches at it best knowing many wondered who the hell I was. The sight of everyone seem to want answers.

"Im glad that you could all make it on such short notice but now I like to introduce Dr. Chinalski from Stanford University, he specialized the Theory of Alien Invasion." Please welcome Dr. Chinalski."

"Thank you Madam President."

"Alien theory, really…parents actually pay hard earned money for their kids to learn this?"

"General Talley, at ease and Dr. tell us what you know of this and all that is going on."

"As we all know of Area 51, well this somewhat revolves around it, if we are invaded." 'Our invaders are more likely to take over earth, all that you know will go blank." 'Our data stream cut entirely alone with communication will ceased as well."

"What about our phones Dr. Chinalski?"

"General Talley…right sir?"

"Read the name tag doc."

"At ease General."

"My apologies to Mr. Theory."

"General their communication is more likely far more advance than ours and they will jam up our cellure communications."

"We have television."

"General Talley, that maybe scramble as well, our invaders have more likely studied our entire history from telegraph to our most current advanced communication we have now." 'They will do their best to prevent any communication among us and they know of our natural fear."

"So they know that we are afraid of the dark."

"General!"

"Its ok Madam President but what I meant General Talley is that they may bring force panic upon our secure way of life, this could be done by sight alone."

"This communication, could our satellites be disrupted, could you speak on that?"

"Madam President, that will be infected but your radio and optical telescopes maybe be able to receive information hopefully." 'But there is no guaranteed but its ancient technology may be overlooked.

"Dr. Chinalski, my soldiers are prepared for the worst."

"General within several hours of an invasion. I hope that your words re so true because they will become our front line defense." 'Fighter Squadron will take to the sky scrambling into action, but for Alien Spaceships that travel thru space with repulsion technology beyond our physics." 'Even if they are fired upon." Their travel maybe twice that of sound or greater that our weapons want even matter to them sir."

"Dr. Chinalski, my name is Major Wick our advance decoding technology, my specialty…what is your opinion?"

"Your technician will try to intercept and destroy their commination while your basic Humvee will broadcast radar dishes targeting Alien Crafts with microwaves hoping to jam their cyber alien signal." 'But its chance of being effective is slim."

"Hey who side are you on here!?"

"Calm down General, he is on our side and we need his professional opinion."

"Yes, Madam President."

"General Talley, you may have your militaries to unleased experimental weapons when everything you have has failed." 'Due to desperation of getting something done Z-001 Air Force Space Fighter but our best will be no match."

"How do you know of this weapon, its top secret very classified!"

"Maybe 15 hours into the invasion, our nation are more likely on becoming one while our invading alien will be working on clearing the skies." 'They will

destroy military targets around the world like radar installations and towers before moving on to attack infrastructures of our own society." 'Our nuclear weapons will be saved for the last Madam President."

"Our…Navy will save this world as we have done before, are you aware of our great history… many victories such as japan." Admiral Thornton said.

"I have had about enough of whomever you are." General Talley shouted loudly."

It was that moment he gotten up walking toward the doctor looking down on him.

"Maybe we need to test your blood and see what you really are." General Talley said aggressively.

"General, be seated." President Hillary ordered.

We watch the Old General just stand there, if looks could kill, there would have been a death among us.

"General, sit your ass down now!" 'That a direct order General!" President Hillary shouted loudly.

It took her to get loud as he walk back to his chair mumbling to himself the entire time.

"Madam President, with time; you may order your Staff to shield bunkers and secret location and General, you may order your Military Officers to issue an order for surprising new tactics." 'Instead of an attacks, they order their forces to run away." Dr. Chinalski explained.

"President, this one is really getting beneath my skin right about now!" General Talley said loudly.

"After 48 hours of the Alien Invasion, it should be complete and the invaders now have control of the skies and ground and the remaining communication cycles around civilians evacuation." 'Panic and desperation now lives among us causing rioting mobs." 'America roadways will grind to a halt and safety from aliens means that subways, tunnels and sewers provide safe exit from burning cities." Dr, Chinalski explained.

"Expert believe that destruction of civilization is predictable from fighting with an Invasion Alien Force doctor but while our military may be defeated, it doesn't end the war." President Hillary said.

"You are right, but among the survivors will grow seeds from human transferring them into killers as they will rebel." 'Survival tactic will spawn from the caves, desert and forest that they took shelter." Dr. Chinalski said.

"Dr what will happen with weeks to come?" President Hillary ask.

"From the first week until several thereafter when our cities are destroyed and remnants are what remain, urban chaos and fail evacuation will kill thousands in the first few days." 'We will scavenge supplies while searching for canned food and clean water along with flash lights, batteries and the basic knife will become valuable." 'But the key to long term survival is teaming up with other peoples." Dr Chinalski

"Our soldiers will survive." General Talley said.

"Maybe General, but you must keep in mind is that, they are peoples first and may stray away from their responsibilities as well as their Units in search of their families and friends, maybe even known associates for whatever reason may exist within themselves." 'Soldiers may take off their uniforms and possible become key leaders of remaining human groups." Dr. Chinalski explained.

"None sense, that hard to believe and you know nothing about loyalty." General Talley responded.

"General, this technology will play no part after the invasion and simple communication devices like walkie- talkie and hand held radios and old telegraph lines will become important." Dr. Chinalski responded.

"What do you think of, let say…6 months later." Secretary of Defense Allison ask.

"We will be force to fight these aliens with low tech guerilla tactics and small scale explosives, the only thing we may have on our side is that the Alien Force may have ventured to far from home." 'They may rely on reinforcements, with everyone lost, they mayn't be able to be replace." 'This maybe their weakness." Dr. Chinalski said.

"How about bacteria." President Hillary ask.

"Survivors will be face with illness from disease and bacteria, lack of antibiotics and other basic medicines." 'But maybe this'll become

our weapon toward our invaders but we maybe more in danger from unknown germs." Dr Chinalski responded.

"How will we be able to defend ourselves overall?" President Hillary ask.

"Everything technology wise required some type of electrical and when that no longer available, man will've to become hunters like the once cave man." 'Our intergalactic invaders want have no need to worry about being invaded with technology and we will have to fight primitive...meaning hot air balloons could become our game changer because of it's so low tech, it may be almost invisible to advance technology, maybe even alien eye sight as well."

"How do you think?" General Talley ask.

"General Talley, coordinated assaults with high explosive and scavenged bombs, throughout history we have use low tech weapons worldwide against superior technology." 'Our victory over their technology may have less to do with tactics and more to do with human spirit." Dr. Chinalski said.

Chapter 7

"AMERICA THREATEN"

Alien Spaceships hover above us spreading themselves out among America and eventually begin to drift but our satellites had detected their Mother Ship a few hundred miles above us. The media was having a fill day with this from CNN to the no name news stations blasting the TV screen like if this was the beginning of time. It was the third day of this madness when the President address the nation. It was nothing no more than bravery at its finest but something had to be done with the quickness.

This country was going crazy, we watch the most powerful woman in the world stand among her battlefield soldiers. Her fiery red hair with blond streaks blew in the storming wind, all that we feared had come true as we known that we wasn't truly alone. But so many feared what we had taking on would come back to haunt us someday, it was nothing more than a worldwide ceremony for everyone to see. The sight was the White House as our President address the nation.

The world thought it was crazy as protesters flooded the streets of immigration building all over the United States. Eventually the White House day's prior but before the big day, the military had been brought in to keep the peace as the protestors stood in the rear. We watch these aliens take an oath of loyalty to the United States of America. It was nothing more than a parade for the world to see.

I believe it was more around election time for him to regain his second term in office as we listen to his speech about this new life forms. He spoke of their travel, it was nothing more than bullsh*t from the beginning as I stood within the presidential circle in silence. I wasn't the only one who had known that this was going to come back on us in the worst way. These aliens escape their world and somehow they crash landed into our world knowing he knew the truth as well.

If the public actually saw their ship they would have been shock because it look as if they had went through a battle zone. But once we gotten to know more about them, we had learned that there navigational system had been badly damage and that what cause them to enter our atmosphere. NASA was so full of sh*t as they claimed it was a meteor storm that knock them so far off course causing them to enter our solar system. Everything happen for a reason I guess but I could be wrong and maybe it doesn't matter because they are here now as this country has done what they could for them.

It was nothing more than a multimillion dollar project, some of the best engineers that this country could offer had been brought in. America had come up with a suitable living housing system for our newly friends. It didn't take long for them to adjust, maybe it was our similar traits. They wasn't much different from us, there spaceship had been study and even I had to swear secrecy before and after.

If broken or found guilty of espionage or giving away information of their technology, it could mean my death knowing these aliens may have brought more harm than good in the long run maybe. This women who stood next to me wasn't in the protection of the White House but she stood frontline with the rest of us while Seattle was looking like a militarized zone. She was gutsy knowing she probably could be taking out without notice or warning of any kind.

The speech that she had giving that day was overwhelming as it penetrated our heart, so many reporters jump on this band wagon. But to hear her words of how this wasn't a joke nor Hollywood trickery from cameras and sound effects or some eccentric jokester with too much money and time. The world was seeing it with their own eyes that we were actually being invaded by this oversized space craft that had to be at least several miles long easily and its height was just truly amazing. Our fears of something so massive that was far beyond our own capability of even building.

I myself could only imagine the technology it took just to travel thru space itself. I had a feeling that this wasn't going to be a good outcome and im sure the rest of the world felt the same. But in reality I could only hope that the millions of peoples not just in America but worldwide found comfort in the most powerful woman in the world. We watch this phenomenon like hawks to it pray hoping that none of this was real but the sight of the darken clouds no longer burn red as this shadow was breaking through little by little.

The peoples who stood looking on started breaking down praying as if this was judgment day and it was God himself coming for the righteous to take them back to heaven. Before our eyes came this massive unknown foreign craft, it was just a while ago this could be seen by the naked eye and only days ago it could be pick up by Russian Satellite System. There was no turning back now, they were here and we could only hope that they were friendly. I watch the Secret Service Agents surround the President, she was almost completely from our sight but her strong will couldn't allow her to see this with her own eyes.

What we thought was only one now had turned into another just to the left of it and then another to the right, both were half it size. But the space it taking up had to be at least 5 miles in length altogether. It was like if they were in some kind of attack formation, it was that moment we saw the President being force away as military move forward. What was our most feared piece of equipment must to seem like a little ants moving about to those Alien Spaceships that now look down on us.

They knew they had complete control as the wind pick up even more like if a storm was forming even more around them. I felt it up close and personal as the mighty wind was forcing me away but I held my ground the best I could. I had to give props to these reporters, fear didn't live within them as they followed the tanks alone with the ground soldiers. I personally think that nothing around me was any match or could even bring them any form of damage.

It was that moment the Fighter Planes appeared from north with tremendous speed as we could see the Helicopters moving away. They now had the room they needed but they continue to hover like if they were studying us. We could see the Fighter Jets flying aggressive patterns around them, it was nothing more than our own air show it seems but not once did they fire a shot. There was a brief moment that I was so close to the General that I could hear him giving orders before he moved away as silence now lived between us.

"Do not fire unless fired upon." General Talley shouted.

Maybe this was the best, for the situation since everyone and there momma had guns including the citizens. It made me think if everyone carried some form of gun on them just for the hell of it in this country. It had taking a moment before the outer two Alien Spaceships broken completely free of the burning storming clouds. They both move like a ground fire teams dropping in attitude while the bigger Alien Spaceship remain almost completely covered by the burning clouds. It like if it was for some kind of protection or something or cover.

I wasn't sure but that what it seem like while the other two now space themselves apart, both Alien Spaceships was now dropping in attitude. It was that moment the U.S. Navy could be seen moving closer to the U.S. Coast Guards who floated off the Seattle Coast Line. It amazing how the unknown can send human into panic mode as we could see almost every yacht off the coast line bay heading toward Canada or southward toward Oregon. I wasn't sure but our ocean had oversize white caps, it was the strangest thing to see but we will knew who was causing this.

I expected this, maybe more knowing the local law enforcement had their hands full from their own traffic getting as far from the city as possible. It was a sight to see if you were into desperation of the worst kind and yet haven't a shot been fired yet. This lasted for several hours, it was like they were playing chess with us knowing they had the element of surprise along with greater technology. It didn't take us long before we enter Seattle watching them get closer to the coast.

The sight of what we assume was the Mother Ship had remain high in the sky very distance from the Seattle Coastline. The smaller one now push inland toward us, it was as if we were in there destruction range hovering over the ocean bay, the waves alone ponded the coastline. Our battleship's was rocking like toys in a bathtub and the kid was the aliens, it was more than what I wanted to see. Our ships pulled away in search of calmer waters it seemed.

The world continue to watch for the next several days as more Naval Battle Ships arriving as well as Army Infantry Units. It wasn't long before the city of Seattle looked like a military base with all that was going on while civilians and citizens were being evacuated. Seattle highways had become congested, jammed to the point of no return while others turned to the churches for protection. The mayor himself spoke of this but he refuse to infringe on religion, even the National Guards kept their distance from churches making it their choice.

So much kayos was happening all at one time that this was even hard to believe if you didn't see it for yourself. It wasn't until 3 days later that the Mother Alien's Ships had broken free of the burning red clouds. The smoke alone drifted over into Canada causing havoc on their population as they line there on border. You could even see their Fighter Jets patrolling alone with ours none stop but even they didn't fire on the alien spaceship.

So much media had made their way to this city to see the Mother Spaceship join the other two that still hovered above the coast line several miles from shore. She sat now between the two and what got the reporter cameras flashing none is when they had all link themselves together becoming one. Maybe they formed a passage of travel for all we know as Helicopters hovered near while our U.S. Navy move in closer once the burning storming clouds was no longer. We will knew that it was cause by them somehow giving them the technology that we didn't have like controlling the weather.

We had been dispatch to return home for mostly my safety as a civilian and to be honest I had no argument with that decision as I wasn't a soldier anymore living for death. My retirement and easy living has silence the once killing wolf that lived inside of me or maybe it was my age of being smarter. The once killer that live in me was now silence, even more so the U.S. Army alone with my government wasn't brain washing my mind anymore. Several more days has come and gone and all I could do was now watch from the distance, what was once silence was no more.

Our invader had launch several small spaceships from Seattle Coast Line without fear and yet not one shot was fired as our Fighter Jets followed there every movement. They flew several missions that had taking several hours at a time for whatever reason and then without notice. We witness what had taking them days to do within minutes as they no longer hover above the ocean off of Seattle Coast Line. They had taking to the sky faster than you could blink your eyes, it was truly fascinating and dangerous at the same time.

Chapter 8

"ALIEN INVASION"

Silence had come about us the next several days but kayos of the city was still just beginning, the citizens believe that the aliens would return. News Reporters had taking what happen and blew it completely out of what was normal but reporters specialized in ousting the truth. I don't blame the citizens of Seattle for not wanting to be a part of what would be the Base of an Alien Invasion. That was how the front page read, it cause nothing but madness from looting to rapid gun sales.

It didn't take long before so many hospitals begin to fill, it even cause city officials and public workers to simply flee with families. Many jobs had been abandon without warning, I guess there protection of love ones was more important. Whatever their reason were, it was understandable, maybe I would have done the same. We were still facing major disruption and according to NASA, our own solar system was being invaded. The world itself was panicking and we were to blame as the aliens that we had taking in had was the cause.

Several weeks had gone by before they resurface about 300 miles off the southern pacific coastline heading toward Los Angeles airspace before sunrise. It didn't take the Navy long to react as they brought their Aircraft Carriers close to the America coastline. Our Coast Guards had done what they could but it was that morning that the entire world watch from their home and mobile technology. It was nothing more than a sight to see as this Alien Spaceship moving from the ocean toward Los Angeles Ca.

I was far from that area but to see it from Washington DC from my assigned motel, I could only imagine what so many imagine while looking up toward the sky. This alien invasion was before all our eyes, our Fighter Jets and Helicopters followed it closely but not one shot was fired while listening to my phone ringing none stop. There was much to say while my television screen was fading in and out but I was still able to see it. But with so much going on, I had other stuff on my mind like heading back to the White House. It didn't take me no time to get their making my way into the heavily protected gate.

The thought of been here more times than I care to remember and ever time, my credential was check like if it was my first time. It was only understandable with so many public threats made toward the President like if this was her fault. The city panic but it was nothing like Seattle that was still in the madhouse, the moment I had gotten there. It was nothing but brass surrounding the President as I was ask to join in on the meeting.

I spent more than 25 years in the U.S. Army and 15 of it was being attach to Special Forces and within my military career. I only taking one picture with the Vice President, it was still a big thing for me to be near such a powerful leader of the world. This right here was completely out of my circle but I was here and who knows, maybe I will be ask my opinion. I could only hope not because battlefield soldier should not play in world politics but then again that was General Mc Author when he ran for President of the United States. Before I had taking a seat, all I heard was.

"What the hell is this now?" President Hillary ask loudly.

This woman wanted answers from the way she was looking at everyone but no one said nothing as she kept looking around the room. Silence had come about everyone, the only sound that was heard was brief cases and papers been fondle back and forth. I could see everyone looking at each other maybe hoping that someone say something stupid or just ay someone period that they could add on to it.

"Come on peoples, we have some of the smartest peoples in our country right here and no one have a simple answer for me." President Hillary ask while yelling.

Once again no once said nothing while glancing at the monitor screen that she had turned on with her remote control.

"NASA…explain to me what is going on and what you think they want."

This woman needed to relax is all I was thinking.

"Madam President, we have been monitoring them for the longest and the minute we saw movement, we contacted you alone with the Navy who track them entering our airspace."

"Ok, I'm aware of that, now tell me something I don't know." President Hillary said mildly.

Silence found it way among us.

"Admiral please give me some good news."

"Madam President, we know just as much as you do, we know that there are two more about 150miles above our planet just sitting there" 'Not once has they separated since they left Seattle as we tried to guess why but we come up with nothing. Admiral Thornton informed her.

"Madam President our satellite system can track their presence and their movement but we can't penetrate their inner system no matter what we do." NASA responded.

"I want more information like why are they heading into the desert and why haven't they made contact with us or why haven't they communicated with us or why is all our technology going haywire!"

"Madam President, my Officers has been giving strict permission not to fire unless fire upon and even then they are to get permission to fire." (General added) *'Madam President we know for sure that it is only three Alien Spaceships and they seem not to have a force field surrounding them."* Air force General Keaton said loudly.

"Ok and how would you know that General?"

"Madam President, from the beginning our Fighter Jets has been firing sound waves that reflect back to us each time we fire upon them." General Talley

That moment everyone gotten quiet, this alone could've been an act of war if there spaceship would have taking this as an attack or aggression. I could do nothing but sit back and listen to everyone get loud with each other, so many now argue as some thought it was the right thing to do while others didn't. It had taking the President to get things back in order, this alone told me that we wasn't working together and it would take much before we be at each other throats.

"If we can't seem to control ourselves than how're we going to control and entire nation especially those with guns?" I said.

"I want to hear from you, what is your opinion of this madness?" President Hillary ask.

The sight of everyone now looking at me as I felt this painful heaviness in my stomach.

"I would like to hear something from you, it is the reason why I requested you here since you were the first to come in contact with our long term alien guest."

"Ms. President or Madam President, well I believe that these aliens are here for as you call our long term guest." I replied.

"Why do you say that, I really want to know?"

"Madam President, I did come in contact with them and for a while I communicated with them, it wasn't long after I found out that they were actually escaping their homeland" "They were slaves Madam President and me being a product of slavery…well I could understand what they were going thru and why they wanted something better." I responded.

Silence had come about the room but it was that second someone busted into the room heading toward the Army General. I couldn't hear what was been said or able to see the envelope he had open. That moment he had gotten everyone attention.

"I gotten some news to share with all of you…it had been confirmed that the Alien Spaceship has touch down Death Valley California in the heart of the desert." General said loudly.

That moment the President had taking a seat at the head of the table looking at all of us while papers was being shuffled around. We watched her get up walking toward the monitor that showed there every movement before looking back at me.

"What do you think they want?"

"Madam President, when slaves would run away from the plantation…it was very rare that the owners would go looking for them." I responded.

"What are you getting at?"

"Madam President, I think they are here for the slaves or they are Alien's Bounty Hunters, either way I don't see nothing good coming of it. I responded.

"Very good observation, maybe I should put you on the payroll or give you some of these stars."

"Madam President, this is the first time in history that we face an alien that maybe be friendly but I sense nothing but hostility." 'They seem to have studied our terrain and chose one of the hottest places in our country, I think this is where they are going to set up their base." I responded.

"Tell me why you feel this way and why?" President Hillary said.

"Madam President, I feel that they know that their knowledge and technology is greater than ours and that they can bring major damage upon us." 'I also fear that if they bring war upon our soil that it just want affect us but the world as a whole." I responded.

"So tell me what you suggest?" President Hillary ask.

"Well, I think we should just give them back but it we do than they know that we are weak and don't want war and if they feel that way…then why wouldn't they just take this entire world." I responded.

It didn't take a rocket scientist for them to figure out that we were the most powerful of all.

"Madam President, we have studied them from a distance and from my observation, maybe they were hovering over our oceans to study the water." 'Maybe they Have taken a liken to our world and want it for themselves and I agree with the gentlemen." Admiral Thornton said.

"I agree as well, if we give in than maybe they see it as a sign of weakness." General Talley added.

"I'm the Secretary of Defense Allison and no one had ask me anything, Madam President…im the 3rd in charge and I say if we come in contact." 'I say we should give them up and let them go home."

"I agree, this isn't some foreign country…these are actually aliens that we know nothing about and we are completely out of our league here. "Vice President Ayla suggested.

This had become a debate that was going back and forth until the President had gotten involve bringing it to an end.

"Gentlemen's, we have heard a lot and all I can say is that we have this alien spaceship on our soil while two others hang above our planet." 'I want each of you to get with your commands and get me answers so I can avoid World War 3." President Hillary said.

This meeting had be adjourn but before it was the President had ask me to stay behind, it was something I never thought.

"Would you like something to drink?" President ask.

I didn't know what to say until I watched her pour herself a mix drink while asking me if I was sure knowing it would be rude if I denied her.

"That would be nice Madam President." I responded.

I watched while she spoke of politics wondering why she kept me behind but it was ok as we talk for a while before leaving.

"You don't mind staying for a while do you?"

"No, sorry Madam President."

"Relax and I want you to spend a few day here in the White House overnight, are you ok with that?"

"Whatever you want Madam President."

It wasn't long before I settle into this house of ghost knowing sleep didn't came easy from one day to the next. Maybe this was expected with so much history but breakfast with the President and sometimes her Staff. It was nothing more than amazing but one morning was unforgettable. Silence had come between us when the President had been brief on the current events of the aliens that seem to taking ground upon our land. She had a few questions regarding the information she had gotten as I listen to several response but I guess she wanted more.

The way she kept glancing at the monitors that displayed there every movement as we could see much but there alien spaceship without movement.

"Mr. Baily…you encounter this Alien Race before anyone".

"Madam President, what I encounter was a friendlier aliens, I have no knowledge of these new invaders." I responded.

"Interesting but tell me something that'll get me to thinking."

"Madam President, you have to be aware that history has taught us that aliens seem to have popped up in human history since ancient times over a thousand years ago, extraterrestrials have landed on earth." 'We even hailed them as gods and some believe that they have helped shape our human civilization.

"So you say they have been here before?"

"Madam President, I do believe history and some of the most famous astrologers have studied such history like Peru's Nazca Desert.

"I'm not familiar with its history, can you enlighten me?" President ask.

"For instance the giant human figures of Easter Island and carvings of Puma Punku in the Bolivian highlands, these're evidence of such invasion of this world humanity." 'I myself could only hope that we learn to accept them or parish before them." I said.

"Another quack." General Talley said loudly.

"Meaning what."

"Madam President you are the key leader of this world and even more so, this is happening on your watch and what you do will make the world itself decide from you." 'If we are to make this work, not that we don't have much of a choice with their technology it. We have to live in green…meaning peace because it'll help the world population participate in this evolution of consciousness with aliens." I explained.

"Why aren't you afraid to speak yur mind?"

"Madam President, I'm sure you have studied my military history and you know as well as everyone here that I travel the world and I have over a hundred confirm kills… Madam President I live with each death that was created for we are all special in Gods eyes." 'I can't afford to not speak my mind with the carrier I chosen and you are no different from me accept you ran for office and gotten elected. I said.

It was nothing but silence.

"Would you like something else?"

"Im fine but thank you President."

"You know a lot about politics."

"Well when you are waiting around to deploy, you can either lift weights or find a hobby on your down time when you are not training." 'My hobby was reading history and I enjoy experimenting with science Madam President.

"Interesting…very well spoken Mr. Baily." President Hillary said.

Silence had come about us once again as we continued to eat breakfast.

"Mr. Baily, are you familiar with the bible?" Secretary of Defense Allison ask.

He spoke mildly but it seem to be aim aggressively toward me, it even cause everyone to pause for a brief second as they waited for my response.

"Somewhat, why you ask Sir?" I ask.

"You place God in your conversation." Secretary of Defense Allison stated.

"Sir, I did and I'm sure you are a religious man and the reason I say that is because most that hold your title in this great country is

religious or they believe in something greater than themselves or some form of afterlife that better than this life we live now." I stated.

No one said nothing, not even the President who was trying to figure out where this was heading.

"The Book of Ezekiel."

That moment I realized what he was doing because he did it several times yesterday but I wasn't going to allow this incest bastard to continue.

"Secretary, I know where you are going because in the Book of Ezekiel alone with Sanskrit if you are not aware, it speaks of flying vessels." *'But with that being said like as in ancient history, alien encounters frequently occur in unknown areas far from civilization."*

"Really, tell us more since you seem to know so much." Secretary of Defense Allison said.

I just gotten quiet because I wasn't here to step on no one toes or take someone job plus it may be better if I said nothing more unless ask.

"Why you stop, I would like to hear more Mr." President Hillary responded.

"Well…one of the most known cases of alleged abduction happen in New Hampshire, the date I believe was on Sept. 16, 1961." 'Two ladies claim they are abducted on a lonely darken road in the chocolate mountains."

That moment the Secretary of Defense Allison said something ignorant but I ignored him until the President told me to keep talking.

"Well as it was told that under hypnosis, they explained how the aliens conducted medical tests for two hours, only to erase their memories of this experience." I said.

"You have such a great insight on fables and stories, now tell us how that story helps us with what is going on or are you one of those who like to hear themselves talk about much of nothing soldier." Secretary of Defense Allison ask.

I said nothing in return.

"What he is saying…Sir, is that these stories give us history and maybe they have been studying us not to conquer at that time but to gain knowledge and save us for themselves later…like now for instance."

"Well-spoken General' we will learn why they are here and we must remain peaceful harmony for the better of humanity." President said.

"Madam President, if I may add for your personnel safety as well as mine."

"You haven't stop yet." Secretary stated.

"Go ahead Mr. Baily." President Hillary said.

"I believe that you'd vacate this area as soon as possible."

"Why is that, are you qualified to give such advice?" Secretary ask.

"Well…Sir, you could stay but as far as the President… you should leave Mam because if they were going to destroy anything, it would be this place first I believe." 'Don't any of you watch television, the aliens like to make aggressive statements like blowing up objects of patriotic pride and define glory?" 'I mean look at some of the most famous alien movies, if destruction of these known places would only stirs up the hornets' nest and no matter what you say…peoples would want to fight back." I explained.

"You really have away with words soldier, maybe you should be in politics." Secretary of Defense Allison said.

"Madam President even you must believe now that the possibility of an aggressive Alien Invasion is entirely possible and if it did." 'It would not end well with us, it would be like Christopher Columbus first landed in America and we all know that, it didn't turn out good for the Native Americans." I said.

"So you are a historian as well." Secretary of Defense Allison said.

"Boys, we are all on the same team here and it looks like we can all learn from each other and you two should learn to play well with each, especially now since im offering him a job as an Analyst to my Staff." 'You want a job?" President Hillary ask me.

There wasn't much I could do but accept while she stood up shaking my hand before breakfast ended.

Chapter 9

"The Flood"

Several days pass and all we done so far was monitor there every movement while the Army has taking control of its surrounding area. We haven't seen their image yet but we manage to pick their movement inside their spaceship. My newly job kept me working within sight of the President, she has giving so many speeches about keeping the peace but since they Have been here, so much has happen. So many airlines has been flying none stop to any country other than this one.

Our own citizens was fleeing like roaches, it reminded me of my childhood living when the light comes on. Food prices has been sky rocketing but that may come to an end with this next upcoming speech about price gauging without notice. It was nothing but normal in so many ways because this was nothing more than a money market for those that wanted to make it. Crime itself was on the rise mostly from the poor who wanted what they couldn't afford.

This was nothing more than Seattle all over but worst because it was happen throughout America, the sad part is that. It wasn't much we could do but try to keep the peace while we waited for them to make a move. There was this strange none stop dust cloud that circled the alien spaceships that we couldn't figure out. There was no visibility what so ever, not even there ship was visible except when there was a strong penetrating wind and even then it was only a glimpse.

They seem to have so much control, even with the surrounding weather but from what we could see is that they were here to stay. It was long after several geologist had shown up on their own for whatever reason. But it was to our advantage because they had discover something that even NASA found interesting not the mention a local bombing range. It had belong to the United State Army, their impact meters that was design to monitor bombs been drop from the sky or the local artillery units shelling the area.

I wasn't far from the President when she had receive the information that all this dust that we had been seeing was from digging into the earth. Creating heavy dust like ash from a volcano clouds, we had so much aerial surveillance. It look like a dog fight movie being made but that had come to a ceased when the military deem this area as a no fly zone. It had taking a moment to enforce it with all the media about and civilians wanted to see what was going on.

It was no more than three days passed, this once dusty dry desert was tuning into some sort of ocean forming from the constant storms. Military camps was at war with this crazy unpredictable strange weather that was destroying them by its self. This water destroyed everything within its path without warning, so many lives was been taking. Shoreline of death was forming, even I had to pull bodies from the rough water that continue smashing into embankments.

Devastation and horror, this was their first hostile aggression toward us, we all wanted to react with fire power but the President continue to keep the peace between us and them. I think it was because we still haven't made physical contact with them yet and I can't even recall how many speeches she has giving about peace and how we are too remained civilized. They Have now been in our world at least a month causing none stop havoc. Our civilians wanted answers but we all knew it had to do with the aliens we had in our custody even though we haven't gotten much information from them yet.

We knew more than what we could release to the public hoping to keep the world from going completely crazy. Even more so with the peoples that had more money than they could spend hoping to control their behavior. **"My alien species in known as a Tyims from some planet call Eyumi and it's as gentle as a plantation house n*ggas." 'But some was put to sleep because of their aggressive explosive behavior from killing their owners without warning."**

That went viral causing citizen's protest out of fear of uncontrollable alien attacks. It wasn't long after the media gotten hold about how some manage to escape their human owners. It gotten worldwide media attention. Not long after I ended up back in another meeting and the President wasn't looking happy.

"Ms. Hillary, what is going on here and this is being shown all over the world, it even brought on a worldwide religious uproar." I busted out saying without warning.

This day had bought nothing good as we ended up in another discussion listening to the President speak about what the hell is going on in her country.

"President Hillary, we must attack now while we are able to!" General Talley said loudly.

"Don't you dare rise your voice at me General, it is very un-call for and it's not needed right now...do you understand me." President Hillary spoke loud and firm but professional.

"My apologies President Hillary but what're we to do but sit and watched them bastards do as they please and why did you hire me... im doing nothing but sitting around." 'I have thousands of hard core killers sitting on bases throughout this country doing nothing but waiting to receive the word go President Hillary." General Talley said somewhat mildly.

"General do you want a war between them and us because if you do than you are not thinking about this world as a whole!" 'I got China-Russia-Germany-Japan and one to many European Nations all breathing down my neck with troops on standby by as well and not one of them is itching for a fight like you." President Shouted.

"President Hillary you hire me because I have a long history of wars, it not that im itching for a war but we have done nothing but flight operations and put soldiers on its outer perimeter." General Talley shouted.

"That rights General Talley and if you send one soldier in without my permission!" 'I will fire your ass and bring you up on disobeying a direct order and not to mention inciting a war...you understand me General!" President Hillary ask aggressively.

"Loud and clear President Hillary…loud and clear mam." **General Talley responded back louder than he should have.**

There was nothing I could say as he leaned back puffing on his cigar looking around with arrogances.

"You are a Geologist right?" President Hillary ask.

"Yes, Mam President representing NASA." He responded

"What have you come up with within the last 48 hours?" President Hillary ask.

"Madam President, my team has come up with a map of the desert and if you can see on the monitor, they chose Death Valleys because it sits in a large bowl and we think that they space craft's requires some form of major cooling for their engines in our atmosphere that's much warmer than out space." This could be why they hover high above and when they did surface, it was upon the ocean and they did this each time before they made their way inland Madam President." *NASA Geologist Mr. Richmond explained.*

"So you saying they need our ocean to maintain?" President Hillary ask.

"From what we come up with so far the answer is yes." NASA Geologist Mr. Richmond responded.

That moment she look toward the Air Force General *Keaton* who had taking control of the first Alien Spaceship wanting to know if what was being said was true.

"Madam President, what we discover about their ship seem to be true because their engines was burnt, maybe they knew nothing about our oceans but we did see how they were trying to repair their engines using a source of ground water I guessing."

"So, this could be there weakness and if it is, we have to find a way to use it to our advantage." President said.

"Madam President, we sent divers from the Navy into the water and what they done was somehow dug deeply into the earth about 200 feet and we know they pumped about 2500 feet down to get ground water and this is what cause the massive flooding. NASA Geologist Mr. Richmond said.

"What will happen if this water continue to flood?" President Hillary ask.

"We believe that it will flood over the bowl that it sit in and destroy farmland and eventually tape into a river system and cause even

more destruction." 'It will cause nothing but kayos as this water find low ground destroying everything in its path." NASA Geologist Mr. Richmond explained.*

"Can we stop it?" President Hillary ask.*

"Madam President, I and my team don't think it'll because the water is now pumping slower according to monitors we place in the water." NASA Geologist Mr. Richmond? Explained.

"Admiral, you have been sitting quiet and now I want you to add something to this." President Hillary said.*

"Madam President, we have been working with NASA and this gentleman here, the Navy is on standby basically as we have dispatch small armored boats into the water." 'They are very self-contained with the latest technology in oceanographic and we have many ships off the east and west coast and currently dispatching several near the Gulf of Mexica and we are in direct contact with Canada and Mexico." "Admiral Thornton explained.

"Madam President, I see you gave funding to California and Nevada to activated its National Guard, my opinion that was nothing but a mistake."*

"Why is that General Talley?" President Hillary ask.

"President Hillary, you don't want a war but you are allowing weekend warriors to play soldier, they are nowhere near trained like regular army with the worst discipline known to man." General Talley responded.*

"You are saying that they are incompetent of keeping citizen in line and protecting property from looters General Talley."

"Yes that exactly what im saying and what happen if they fire and trigger a war between them and us." General said.*

"Well, General Talley I guess you have job to do to get them up to speed as you meet with your Officers right." President Hillary responded.

This meeting had come to an end but I was ask to stay behind alone with the Army General, I could see it in his eyes that he nor the Secretary of Defense Allison didn't approve of me joining them to Death Valley. I guess it really didn't matter what any on them thought because she was the boss.

"Madam President, may I speak openly to for a brief moment?" I ask.

"You may but does this have to be spoken to me alone?" President Hillary ask softly.

"No Mam, it doesn't." I responded.

She told me to say what was on my mind but the moment I did, she just look at me before getting up walking around looking at the monitor and what was going on. There was so much flooding…FEMA alone with the Army Corp of Engineers and the Navy even deployed there Seabees to help control the water but with the rate it was going, the entire Death Valley Desert would be flooded in a matter of months and with all our technology, there was nothing we could do.

"You will have your duties, I suggest you get to it and I want to see all of you back here in 2days with a full report of what you think." President Hillary said loudly.

She stood there looking at us until we gotten up finding our way to the door that she personally open up for us. She stop me for a brief moment whispering in my ear as I notice both men's stop looking at us knowing from the way they were looking. They was wondering what she was saying to me.

"You have some big ball soldiers." General Talley said.

I just looked at him while listen to the Secretary of Defense Allison tell me that if im going to play this political game that I had to learn the rules to it. I told him that this county is in a world of shit and if we don't do something about it fast that we were all going to be buried deeply in it.

"Listen soldier, we are leaving in one hour, have a light travel bag pack and wear something other than that suit, you look like a politician." General Talley said.

I done what I could to prepare myself, this Marine had even loan me a complete battle uniform, it wasn't what I wanted but it was available. For the longest I thought the Secretary of Defense Allison hated my presence but it was him that had brought it to me and of course like all politicians. He found a way to weasel his way out of the flight by sending someone else in his place. It was ok because he didn't need to be tagging alone anyway.

This was the type of man that would send an entire unit into a mission knowing they had no chance in hell of survival. And im sure he would not lose a wink of sleep afterward, probably would not even visit the outcome… coward-ness at its best. It wasn't long after I found myself in flight on our way to Death Valley, this was going to be a long flight as we left the Air Force Base in a C-135 Cargo Plane. There was no comfort in this monster what so ever but we had a full load of supplies for the ground troops who was constantly moving farther away from the Alien Camp Sight.

It was nothing but none stop flooding as we had arrived at Marshall Air Force Base only to be chopper in to Death Valley. We hover high above looking down at what was nothing more than disbelief, it looked like an ocean of water.

"General Talley, where is that town that sat near." Some young unknown politician ask.

"Son the town is gone, most of the peoples got out but over hundreds of them died, mostly the elderly." General Talley spoke sadly.

"At least they don't have to see the outcome of this, sometimes death is your best medicine, sh*t we are still here to deal with this." "The dead has no more worries about living, especially now." I responded.

Everyone looked at me for a brief moment not saying a word, they must to thought I was a heartless mutha f*cker but it was alright. I see more death than any of them, maybe the General as well and even if he did. We continue to circle this devastation for a while before General Talley ordered the pilot to head toward the spaceship. We hesitated until we gotten authorization from Death Valley Base Command. The closer we gotten, this thing look like it was made for war. We were even right above it and nothing had happen to us.

"This is normal General Talley, I know it's hard to believe isn't it." Helicopter pilot shouted.

General said nothing as he look on alone with several others with disbelief.

"I seen enough, take me to the Commanding Officer of this mess!" General Talley shouted.

We ended up touching down several miles from the two alien spaceships, the sight of the soldier directing us had brought back my military days of coming from a mission. The moment we step out it was nothing but a dog and pony show all over when they saw the stars, these young soldiers acted like if they were in boot camp all over. It amazing how peoples act when they see a few stars along with his entourage of lower officers and enlisted members. I myself would have never thought I would be a part of something like this.

Sh*t I can remember when I was drunk off my ass daily and now im a part of the Presidential Staff, it's really is amazing how the world can turns in the blink of an eye. But I guess im not complaining to much as we touch down and gotten out.

"Good afternoon General Talley. Major Anderson said.

"Good morning, im not in the mood for small talk… who is in charge of this mess?" General Talley responded.

"Sir that would be Lt. Col Greenock." Major Anderson said quickly.

"Well are you going to take me to him or should I wait for him Major" General Talley ask.

"Very sorry sir, please follow me past this control point, this way General Talley." Major responded.

That moment we follow Major Anderson along with entourage into what was nothing more than a cluster f*ck of a tent city with more units that was needed. But who was I to judge this operation, we are been invaded and they was right here looking us in the face. Once we had arrived.

"General Talley, if you could please stand for a brief minute or two while I let the Lt. Col know that you have arrived." Major Anderson said quickly.

I had taking a moment to walk back outside to take a look at what was really going on, so many civilians alone with contractors seem to outnumber the military personal. Every branch was here accept for the Coast Guard and Marines as I wondered back inside noticing the General must be talking with the Lt. Col about what was going on. I stood by until some young Sgt who ask me to follow him as we made our way inside, there wasn't much being said. I already didn't know but even I was amaze that they let us get this close to the spaceship.

"May I ask a question Lt. Col Greenock?" I ask.

It was that moment the General and his entourage look my way giving me approval.

"Lt. Col Greenock and I hovered above looking down at swimmers in the water swimming right next to the Alien Spaceships, how is that possible to get so close?" I ask.

"Well soldier, we have been monitoring their behavior and since we haven't shown hostile aggression, they don't seem to fear us" 'Those divers you saw are Navy…Explosive Ordinance Units alone with other specialized civilians divers exploring that entire area." 'We haven't come up with much yet." Lt. Col Greenock explained.

We were shock that they allowed us to come in contact with their alien craft like that and this meeting lasted a bit longer than we expected. But the General gotten shock when he found out that he was staying here for two more days, even I didn't know.

"This is nothing but horse sh*t." General Talley shouted to his entourage.

We had been shown our sleeping area but it didn't last, I guess the General was right when he told us not to unpack nothing. None of us knew how he done it but within an hour time we could see the Death Valley Camp from the air. We were headed to March Air Force Base for the night and I couldn't wait to eat something hot but even I gotten a surprise that night. Waking up to the comfort of a woman as I walked her out, there stood the General appearing from thin air.

She seemed embarrassed knowing I scan the area pretty good before giving her the ok to leave although he said nothing. I could only think what he thought as she strolled by him slowly with her head down like some little girl who gotten caught by her daddy. Sh*t with all this negativity im sure he was happy for us wondering if my wars stories impress her. My military career took me all over the world and females no matter where they are at never seem to change. That day turned into two and it seem like the General didn't seem to care about what was beyond this safety zone. We eventually return home and I imagine how his report was going to look along with the Secretary of Defense Allison but I guess that wasn't my lane to worry about right now.

Chapter 10

"ASTRONAUTS"

Several days passed when the aliens had deployed several crafts to March Air Force Base' that area had already being on the highest alert. We saw and to see 3 Spaceships hovering above the Base was nothing but unreal. Our aircrafts was already in the air flying above circling the area waiting for something to happen while we could see one of them touching down. The other two hung high above but we couldn't believe what we saw walking out from the craft.

Several astronauts exited walking into an open field, this had all been recorded as we watch them take back to the sky and vanished within seconds. Even I couldn't believe this one but it just happen before my own face. There was no way that we could even think about matching their speed anyway possible, it wasn't only seconds later that medical help was been dispatch to them. The military had taking custody of them including the 2 foreign astronauts.

It was about the 3rd day when I was with the President along with her Staff when we visited what we thought didn't exist anymore. All this time they had been taking captive and that following day we gotten them back. The Russian wanted their astronauts back immediately and we had no choice but to return both of them. I ended up leaving back home wondering about the nightmares that they must to have experience every way possible.

We were even more shock to see them been returned in one piece but who knows how much mental damage has been done to them but time was going to give us that answer. Several more days pass and nothing about none of this has made our citizens life any easier. The media had caught every glimpse concerning the astronauts causing not just our country but the world in general to become irrational. So many shows pop up about abductions causing many to voice their opinions placing fear around the world.

Demographics didn't discriminate according to well-known Investigator and Motivational Speaker describe how aliens will even reject us if we have serious medical conditions. Dr. Randal even spoke of how they want perfection, so they may study our reproductive organs. I found myself watching this one late night show that I thought would have been a waste of my time but with all that has happen. This young man had been ask why he wasn't taking by this Alien Species over 25 years ago.

"I was rejected because I had undergone a vasectomy and it could also be because people my age are less likely to have "harmonic" or reproductive activity going on." He spoke with tears in his eye.

"Maybe you dream this and why you come forward now Mr. Keaton?" Late Night host Byron ask.

"I dream nothing, you think im stupid, maybe you are stupid… maybe all you are fools!" 'I tell you that aliens came to my home during a heavy storm and stripped me down to bare ass and studied my body with advance glowing probes that didn't exist in our time zone…well maybe now they do smarty pants…why are you hosting?" 'You can't get a real job you loser!" Mr. Keaton shouted.

"Ok, calm down…kids maybe watching but Dr. Stanton, is this man mentally delusional or what?" Late night host Byron ask.

I watched this doctor move around in his seat while studying this nut case who kept interrupting the entire time.

"I would not say that he was mentally disturb, but some of the things I have heard him say about how he was abducted in Vietnam." 'During a heated battle just before what would have been his death and alone with him constantly saying gook on national televise show." Doc said.

"Then tell us what you think of this nut case." Late host Byron ask.

"I have observe this young man and I would like to share that although abductions and other UFO-related incidents do tend to favor

adults, sometimes children's and often these abductees have family members who've reported having abduction experiences." 'Now with this military involvement could've been created and to this man…in his mind…this is real." 'It a normal among claimants psychological characteristics." Doc explained.

"So this man is a real nut case and he can get a check?" Late night host Byron ask loudly.

"That not what I meant, this man maybe suffering from psychopathology prevalence and maybe prone to "mildly paranoid thinking," nightmares and having a weak sexual identity and psychiatric illness."

"So, Doc, he need to get laid and quick!" Late night talk show shouted.

The audience found this to be more comedy than something that should be on the more serious matter.

"No that not what I'm saying, ok, for instance… several Astronauts returned to us only days ago and I was presence during their interview." 'Now we will know that they were abducted because we saw their return to us… these astronauts experience pro-abduction at a higher level of paranormal activity occurrences from independent corroborating to psychic multiples personalities symptoms." '1st they were captured to a point that they were incapable of resisting, and taken from their terrestrial surroundings to an apparent Alien Spacecraft." 'They were giving examination and invasive physiological and psychological procedures alone with simulated behavioral situations, training & testing, or sexual liaisons." '3rd they were place in isolation and question telepathically and in their native language." 'These abductees were given tours of their captor's vessel and taken multiple places inside strange unknown Alien Craft or maybe more." Doc said.

"What does those men's of glory have to do with this nut job here?!" Talk show host Byron ask somewhat loudly with laughter.

"What this man is saying could be similar to those astronauts I interview because often abductees often forget rapidly the majority of their experience, either as a result of fear, medical intervention, or both." 'And just as this man said how he was return in civilian clothes other than the uniform he was wearing when they took him." Doc said.

"This crack pot said he return inside the White House!" Late night talk show host Byron shouted.

Everyone just look on in silence, it was strange it seem.

"Abductees who are returned to earth are occasionally returned in different locations from where they were allegedly taken un-injured or with new injuries or disheveled clothing." 'They may have a profound mystical sense of love while experiencing oneness with God with the universe, or their abductors." Doc explained.

"So you saying that he is not a nut sickle?" Late night host Byron ask.

"This man maybe experiencing a metaphysical change and he should not be scrutinized but you must help him cope with the psychological and physical from what he experience socially." Doc said.

"You telling us that we need to take this Cracker Jack…serious?" Late night host Byron ask.

"What this man experience maybe may have been orchestrated or predetermined abduction experience, these feelings manifest compulsive desire but yet familiar unknown severe feeling will soon occur." 'Abductees faces anxiety that may last a lifetime forcing him into complete absent." Doc said.

"Doc me nor have anyone here understood a word you have said, can you speak normal English, maybe you are nuttier then this fool!" Talk show host Byron said loudly.

He sat there in silence looking from his nerdy looking glasses with his plaid high water pant, this man needed to a serious make over.

"Trauma is what abductee experience alone with psychological posttraumatic stress disorder syndrome, it put them in some form of altered state of consciousness." 'British abduction researchers called this the Oz Factor because it limit self-willed mobility." Doc said.

"What're you talking about now Doc, once more no one knows what the hell you are talking about?!!!" 'My audience is falling asleep because of you Doc" Talk show host Byron ask.

Even I had enough of that crazy doctor, he was just a nuttier than the idiot he was talking about as I grab another beer before going to bed. I eventually laid down and fallen asleep. I had a long day tomorrow as I had awaken to the smell of morning coffee, all I had to do now was put some water on my ass before the house and hit the roach coach.

"Hey Pedro, I will take some of your rat burritos and that salsa from the can."

I watched his every move knowing for some reason this man only like one thing about me and that was my money.

"Here you are and like I told you, my name is Jose... can you say Jose, that my name...not Pedro. He said loudly.

"Ok, Juan Gonzales Beto." I responded.

That Pedro is making all kind of money right now, especially with so many living in fear of being abducted or attack. Nothing else is open accept for these Mexican roach coach and Asian food of all sort, American are nothing more than sh*t talking weasels hiding behind anything possible. It had only taking me a moment to get to the White House and from the looks on the President face, this wasn't the face I wanted to see. It was too early in the morning as I sat silence trying not to make awkward noise with this cheap wrapping paper.

I eventually sat it to the side when everyone had begun taking notice to me.

"What the hell just happen last night and how in the world was that ghetto talk show host Byron the fool gotten on the air, when it was my strict policy to keep him and other like him off the air!" 'And that Psychologist I want his ass in my office ASAP so I can personally tell him how much of an idiot he was for talking about classified information." President Hillary shouted.

"Madam President, he must to have slip through the cracks somehow as I personally had my Staff to contact every major broad casting agency there was in the country." FCC Advisory stated.

"Mr. Wellman...right?" 'What about the small one like idiot Herbert Wilson Show last night.

He said nothing back as he sat looking away from her for a brief second listening to her only, I guess I don't blame him, this woman wasn't the one to piss off.

"Are any of you aware that im about to go nationwide to talk about abduction because our citizen are afraid to leave there home and when they do, it only to buy food and guns?" 'We have people

doing home invasion taking whatever they want because there isn't enough police to be everywhere, do I have to activate the U.S. Army to patrol our streets or should I declare Marshall Law over nothing and that big mouth Herbert Wilson just sent everyone more into a panic." President Hillary said loudly.

Silence had come about us for a brief moment before this hot intern had come to let the President know that she was going public in 5 minutes. I personally thought she was too emotional but being Commander in Chief, she was nothing more than an actor herself as we listening to her another minute before she went public. She spoke with honor and courage.

"I will activate the National Guard and if that not enough, than the regular military to keep the peace." President Hillary said loudly.

It wasn't long after, I thought she would have ended the meeting but it didn't happen as we watched her say goodbye to the world. She ended speaking to the world for a moment of silence and I had been told by one of her Advisors that the meeting will continue.

"Sorry for the inconvenience for that moment I had to address the nation." President Hillary said.

It was that moment we all gotten comfortable again as he said she just need a better understanding of abduction.

"Well, Madam President, many stories has been documented about Alien Abduction and there tend emphasis is on the human anatomy mainly for scientific examination and routine diagnosis." 'Often for medical purposes due to our unfamiliar study purposes." Dr. Jane Mc Quire said.

"Define medical purposes." President ask.

"Alien tend to have interest in our cranial and nervous system, reproductive system, cardiovascular system, respiratory system below the pharynx and the lymphatic system, they may ignore the upper region of the abdomen and often they do not wear gloves." Dr. Jane Mc Quire explained.

"So you say that we may become experiment?" President Hillary ask.

"Yes, lot of abductee has said how they are force to drink liquids and take unknown pills and giving ejection and some have mention things call tongue depressor." 'examination tend to focus on sex and

reproductive biology and there examiner tend to be taller or a different species altogether." Dr. Jane Mc Quire said.

"What happen after these so call medical exam?" President Hillary ask.

"Alleged abductees have reported that procedures being performed with entities while been forced to view screens display of images with intent to provoke certain emotional responses." 'They often force hallucination like mental visualization or illusionary scenario like roll playing." Dr. Jane Mc Quire said.

"Describe to me this scenario and why?"

"Aliens often uses hypnosis, to relax while studying your state of consciousness, often to stimuli you to face-to-face conversation." 'Aliens want to repress your memories and emotions, often producing headaches and unexplained physical symptoms." Dr. Jane Mc Quire said.

"Are you aware of the seven steps?" President said.

"Madam President are you referring to how abductees tend to seek out hypnotherapist as they try to resolve unusual phenomena patient lives cause by imagery enhanced distortions" 'But first there are four, there is the conference that consist of interrogation session and ten there is the tour" 'It consist of harshness rigor physical mostly medical examination and the journey as abductees reported traveling around the earth or experiencing ruthless planets and terrible species known for extensive medical probing before returning." Dr. Jane Mc Quire said

"What are the other three?" President Hillary ask.

"Sometimes abductor make mistake when returning captives like returning to them to unknown areas of the world." 'Realization of a phenomenon that victim actually believe that it is their fault and this is when support groups tend to bring them back to reality." Dr. Jane Mc Quire explained.

"Describe professional help they may need?" President ask. "This country alone with Canada and Australia seem to be hot spots for abduction and often these abductee need years of professional help from experience psychotherapy." Dr. Jane Mc Quire explained

"What are the norm that these abductee will suffer from? "President Hillary ask.

"Hallucination and temporary schizophrenia, epileptic seizure, parasomnia and near sleep mental-ness like hypnogogic night terror paralysis." 'They also tend to be demonological and everything in

between, it like they Have this unknown mystery within themselves."
Dr. Jane Mc Quire said.

"Mystery huh, define please." President said.

"They often experience frission of terror, even from reading ghost
stories or watching horror movies or fear been put under hypnosis from
fear of being kidnap or being unaware of their surroundings." Dr. Jane
Mc Quire explained.

"This has been more than interesting Dr. Jane Mc Quire has giving me
much better understanding, especially if I have to speak to the media." 'Are
you all aware of the disappearance that we have been getting lately?" President
Hillary said.

I was more than happy to hear her end this meeting, it was putting me
a sleep more than anything but I wasn't the only one it seem.

Chapter 11

"War Declared"

This was a day that was never going to be forgotten no time soon as I rushed to the White House along with the General and his entire Staff. I always knew something like this was going to happen, it was only a matter of time with so many on the highest of alert. The soldier that was supposed to be nothing more than state warriors trained for natural disasters and riot control was now playing a major part in this invasion. We all sat talking among ourselves while drinking coffee and eating bake donuts, if it wasn't for what happen. This treatment made me feel like royalty while listening to brief conversations among the key military leaders.

"Attention…on your feet's." Marine Gunny Sargent yelled loudly.

Commander in Chief had walked in and she didn't look happy at all but it was expected is all I can say as she walked toward the monitor first. Silence had come about the oval office, it was as quiet as a mouse for the first time since I been here this morning. We watch her walk around the room looking at each of us saying nothing but she took a strong look at me. Maybe she remember what I had told her about how top politicians should stay in their lane and leaving the battlefield decision to the Battlefield Generals.

We will have our jobs, the military taught me to be survivor and killer, to put me behind a desk and make me an overnight paper pusher is completely out of my lane. I want be effective or good at this job.

"Lt. Col Greenock are you aware that I have been keeping the peace but it wasn't just me, it was the General here, it was the Admiral here,

it was my Staff that you see here!" 'Now tell me why on your watch that you just pushed us into World War 3...can you tell me?" President Hillary ask.

Silence had come about the Oval Office.

"We have a war going on beyond these walls that alone means that im waiting for an answer would be nice Lt Col. Greenock

"Madam President, I enforce all your rules and regulations but you have no knowledge of what was it is all about." Lt. Col said mildly.

"Really, then why don't you tell me what war is all about?" Lt. Col Greenock.

"Madam President, it was an incident that happen with National Guard Soldiers that fired heavily upon a Patrolling Alien Spacecraft." Lt. Col said.

"I know what happen Lt. Col Greenock, infect let me show you the video of the aftermath of what happen on your watch." President Hillary said.

It was that moment she gotten up walking toward the monitor turning it on, we couldn't see the actual shooting of the Alien Spaceship. But what we were looking at was even worse, the swimmers that had been out there probing around the Alien Craft. They all died instantly like if they were electrocuted, they even open fire on the surrounding boats within the area. We fought back but they were no match for their explosive fire power and nothing but death had come from it.

Our vessels burned afloat until they sunk while some of our men's fought the death that wanted them, the aliens didn't allow them to escape. They died helpless in the water screaming and yelling until they were heard no more. But the alien fire power pushed inland destroying everything within their sight. Our military fought back bravely but they wasn't prepared for such a massive release of unknown weapons upon them. That entire Death Valley Camp was nearly destroyed with only a few survivors. We watch the President turn it off.

"Lt Col Greenock, during this massive invasion... where was you at during this slaughter?" President Hillary ask aggressively.

Silence had come about the room once more, it was like if he didn't want to answer the question that had been ask by the Commander in Chief.

"I want an answer Lt. Col of your ware about when your Camp was being destroyed. President Hillary ask.

I so wanted to say something but like the Secretary of Defense Allison had told me if I was to survive in this game. I had to know how to play this game and know when to shut my mouth.

"Lt. Col...answer now please!" President Hillary ask.

"I had taking my wife to Calienta Resort." Lt. Col said lowly.

"Where is that for us that never heard of that place?" President Hillary ask.

"It an Island outside of Los Angeles." Lt. Col said with the same tone of voice.

"Gentlemen what we have here is a Lt. Col who plays by his own rules and don't care to follow the rules I set forward." President Hillary said.

This woman knew nothing about war, she was completely out of her lane right now and maybe it was the charge alone. Sometimes there is no answer but sh*t happen in conflict zone.

"Lt. Col Greenock do you have anything to say for yourself as to what happen and where do we go from here because I would really like to know?" President Hillary ask.

"Madam President, we were only the edge of war...this could've happen at any given moment within the blink of an eye" 'It sad that my Camp gotten completely destroyed alone with those sailors and civilians and those in small boats." 'This wasn't supposed to happen like this as I teach all my Officers to maintain peace and respect the Rules of Engagement that been set forth under the Geneva Convention of War." 'I can't change what has happen but our soldiers fought back and with that been said, 10 Alien Crafts had been destroyed and now we have possession of those Spacecraft." 'We now know that they can be defeated and they are subject to death...meaning that we can't do nothing but learn from this." Lt. Col Greenock said loudly.

He was right as she stood looking at him and even those out ranking him knew that he was right about everything just said.

"Lt. Col Greenock, was it your goal to become a full bird Colonial before you retire?" President ask.

"Madam President, that is my goal to make Colonial and beyond." Lt. Col Greenock said.

That moment she walk over to her area picking up some darken file.

"Lt. Col...I see that you are up for promotion but that not going to happen no time soon or at least if im in Office." 'In fact I want your resignation right now." President said.

"Madam President, only Congress can demote me or a Superior Officer and seeing that you are neither...this is not your lane." Lt. Col Greenock said loudly.

That moment she walk over to the General and demanded that he be Court Martial for Deliration of Duty under the UCMJ.

"Madam President, this matter can be handle in a different way... Lt. Col Greenock is a good Officer and we can discuss this later, we need every good man for this war we are in...he is highly decorated and has been giving many awards by 3 Presidents and receive the Medal Of Honor, we can discuss him later." 'I say this with respect Madam President.

"Lt. Col Greenock, you are dismiss from this meeting and you are to return to your Base and confine to your Quarter for now, this is a direct order from your President."

He sat there looking like some a boot camp soldier before coming to his feet's looking at the General who had nodded at him. It was like if he giving him the approval to agree.

"Yes Madam President." Lt. Col Greenock said.

He saluted her before leaving, this was nothing but a sad moment because this was the Soldier of Soldiers and no one is perfect. But to take a battlefield soldier from a war is nothing but ignorant, I know because I have found my ass in hot water many of times.

"Madam President, may I voice my opinion." I ask.

She stood there saying nothing at first but as I sat next to the Secretary of Defense, I felt him bump my leg while shaking his head. Maybe he was right about me not saying nothing as I look at her and said that it was ok.

"Moving on from that, we are now at war with an Alien Species that we know nothing about, it's time for ideas and answers." 'I want opinions of how we are going to defeat there technology?" President Hillary ask.

"Silent had come over all of us because known of us had answers for what she wanted to know.

Chapter 12

―∽◦∾―

"Operation Prison Storm"

―∽◦∾―

There was so much was going on with America, it wasn't just a presidential problem but all of ours as a whole and the only outcome, wasn't going to be good. Our leaders had been gather together at the White House, I was there when the President had giving them a task to come up with a solution. It was the first time I saw her actually ask for help without wanting to control everyone and everything thing round her, it was a sight to see. So many defensive plans had been put together enable to protect our country.

Our world was on the brink of an major invasion and with so many ideals, it was to no one surprise that she shot 99.9 percent of them down accept for one, it came from some Congressman child that she was related to.

"You could just use the prisoners, like the ones I see picking up trash on the road sometimes." Little girl said.

"Honey please keep the noise down, grownups are talking." Congressman Todd Evangelist said lowly.

That moment everyone just look over at this 10 year old child playing with some stuff animals, she shouldn't have even been in here but in reality, it made so much sense. I saw the look in the President eyes when she look down upon her.

"Is that possible?" President Hillary ask.

"Madam President, are you sure this is what you really want to do?" Vice President Ayla ask.

"Do you have a better ideal?" President Hillary ask.

"Well, not at the time but to use prisoners as a fighting force, what guarantee do you have that they will kept loyalty to this country." Vice President Ayla stated.

"Vice President, this ideal had come from a child and I believe that it will work and until you sit in this in my chair, you don't have to like my ideals or the decision I make but you will at least respect them." President Hillary said.

We all looked at each knowing I Vice President Ayla wanted to voice her opinion while twirling the end of her braids. Im sure we all thought why not use the inmates for an invasion but maybe it was better that the Vice President leave this one alone. But she was just as strong minded as the fiery red headed herself.

"Now that what I want to hear, we have some of the smartest peoples in the world and yet it takes a child to solve out problem." 'I want this to happen now and I don't care how you do it, I don't care what kind of deals you make with them to make this happen."

"Madam President, we could ask for volunteers first, they usually make the best soldiers since we will be trusting these men with firepower." General Talley said.

"General, first you must make them believe in themselves to start with…meaning you will be calling them soldiers and nothing more, no inmates or crooks because that how they willl act."

"Madam President, I have been training soldiers since you were in diapers, I know how to treat them from beginning to end." General Talley said.

These two seem to have a war of their own but if it wasn't for this invasion, im sure she would have fired his ass by now. Maybe when this is all said and done, it will be her gift to him, it wasn't long after we ended this day. But within the next two on coming weeks… Operation Prison Storm developed but it wasn't until several months later. It was official and I can still remember the headlines as it went worldwide before it's time.

But I guess nothing like that goes un-notice no matter how hard you try, it was bound to get out the moment the first prisoner had been released over to the government. America was nothing more than the country of yackers from beginning to end, even more so from everyone on this gravy trained of free money. But that all had come to an end with time and the world cheered out struggles. America was hitting rock bottom as this intensified this so call invasion that was waiting to take place upon us.

Foreign Spies made their way into our land searching for information but with this it produce mercenaries in search of quick profit. It didn't matter what their motive was and I had privilege of watching some of these unforgettable tactics. So many screams of pain and torture and females was worser than the men's when it came to getting information of any kind needed. This country was becoming unbearable to live in safety from the one too many overnight trained killers that was sent for nothing no more than war and destruction.

So many eyes had been open as what was once America Allies now had become enemies and faced nothing but death. It was nothing but brilliance at its best as America deployed hundreds of thousands upon countries around the world. While remaining defensives as our prisoners fought hard upon foreign land that they destroyed from the air sea and land killing everything in sight. I guess when you pushed someone into a corner, they Have no choice but to come out fighting when all else is lost.

So many decorations should have been giving out but the ones who manage to live through theses many invasions around the world. Some volunteered for a second chance at life and some even came for citizenship or opportunity of killing including our own American. We were at war with nations around the world knowing others nation look as us like barbarians while protesting. So much was going on while facing an alien invasion that we knew was coming our way and it wasn't until a year.

We all sat down coming together with a ceased fire agreement bringing our ignorance to as stand still knowing our invaders monitored us the entire time. We as the world had become our own worst enemies, monkeys were smarter than us right now. Peace had come between us but it didn't last because troops from around the world invaded us without warning. Our homeland for the first time burn like the countries we brought death upon.

But many invading foreigner often found themselves in a bowl of shit as American fought back, it was an awful time and our President had her hands full. So much death had taken place before United Nations had come together due to threats of nuclear war. This ignorance had become worldwide money pit, our own soldiers was being paid with promise to pay notes. With so much going on since our first alien arrival nearly 10 years ago including now, America has been on the verge of bankruptcy.

Rumors was that the remainder of wealth was in reserve status or the next great war knowing I could only hope that it's only political rumors floating about. I remember the first invasion of our prisoner soldiers been uniformed. Many thought we would use ships planes but it was the opposite as we deployed them according to their nationality and their language.

We empty our prisons with many false promises and large sum of money once they return home turning them into assassin of the worst kind. Most work side by side with other hired guns as some of these men's were perfect soldiers. But their choices in life took many opportunities of becoming productive citizens, their existence was classified. We deployed them into places like Russia-China- British Empire-France-Italy- Germany-Japan-Saudi Arabia other Nations that had threaten us.

They were all trained for specific assignments to attack certain locations bringing destruction upon foreign land. It didn't take them long to figure out betrayal and been lied to from the beginning, even I knew that they were never coming back. Some had even become doctors as they learned how to removed poison capsule injected in their bodies. It was nothing more than sadness knowing I help trained some of them from the beginning.

Many just wanted what the government promise them, this alone hunted me knowing I had knowledge of their outcome. Nothing about this world was truly fare and often we are put in situations to make change and like myself I do nothing. Now I see why many countries hate the very ground we walk on knowing we were the most powerful country in the world. It took an incurable virus to break into the inner core while destroying all that we are. The big sleeping giant hasn't awaken yet because too many political games is been played as I speak.

I think of the many times I was far from home alone while depending on others to watch my back as I did theirs. It was like all the theories had come into reality and so many wanted to see us go down for the count with no possible way of getting up. Our technology was far more advance than any country we had ever invaded within our history. But this time it wasn't about that when you had a billion ant's that develop from a grain of rice into the future structure of human anatomy.

They were now big enough to be feared, just like science and medicine changes with evolution. Our President went on national television and promise America a better world was coming with each sunrise. I stood watching wondering with all going on, who were actual believing this b*tch knowing I shouldn't be thinking like this. She is the most powerful women in the world as I felt shameful when she looked my way while giving her speech.

It was as if she knew what I was thinking maybe if I wasn't so corrupted and living for greed. America was turning into a country of have-nots and regulators and hired assassins and our politicians lack morals. It was like we had taking on a curse while breaking a million mirrors and crossing one to many black cats.

During the invasion, so many countries had come for some form of revenge but the two might oceans and neighboring countries…Canada from the north and Mexico from the south. It didn't seem to mean much from the way we deployed Marine Reserve along the northern border and the Army National Guard to the south. So much fighting ripped through both like a hot knife to frozen butter. There was much resistance but like invading ants, eventually number will break through even with the most advance technology.

Allies that we depended on for protection turned their heads when a more powerful advance alien race threaten their own existence. It was like we were extermination our own world while these aliens done nothing but watch from above or monitored from depths that we couldn't reach. Crop-circles that we thought had been done by pranksters was nothing more than aliens mapping our world. We couldn't even destroyed them as they had become their main focus point for land operations.

We didn't have much of a defensive system from entering or taking over what they wanted but we knew it would not be long before gun fire begin. It will be the turning point of this invasion causing us to adjust from a defensive to offensive position. But with that been said, it was never going to be hard to forget how Iraq-Bulgaria-Australia-Germans-France-Russia. Archangel didn't seem to exist among us during the many battles that followed within that year.

Our own military bases along with supply routes were heavily guarded but at the same time, it didn't stop the intense heavy battles that was now taking place. Many of our own fought dame near a losing battle from our alien invaders and the stories about being taking captive was nothing more than a living nightmare. Many of our soldiers had taking sworn oath to take each other lives if that should ever come about. Im a soldier and in many ways I don't blame them from what I have seen one they Have no more use for you.

I remember being shot down while trying to evade the death that was coming our way, we had been hit from the rear knocking out our engine. The sound of mayday could be heard as we listen to the pilot shout out our grid cordinance. I could see nothing while taken on the sight of the thick snowy tree landscape knowing we were about to disappeared into the jungle. It was nothing but our own luck as we barely escape the death that wanted all of us.

We had no choice but to keep moving as they fired none stop burning the forest to nothing all around us as we were in this unfamiliar area. This area was unknown to all of us but we moved without fear until we stumble upon a small farming village while freezing to death. But at least we were alive as we made it into their protective area. This place was so far off the radar and the way they came out like ghost carrying guns surrounding us.

"Lay down your guns." I ordered my soldiers.

It would have only taken them a second to take our lives in the blink of an eye while moving closer to us until they realized who we were. Their leader had giving us our weapons back, it wasn't long before we realized that it was more of them than we thought. They appeared from thin air, there humble attitude along with the way they welcome us was something to remember, food and shelter had been giving. So many women was about them as they had remain unspoken while keeping their distance from us the entire time.

Maybe it was best that we made no connection with them whatsoever especially among us 6 men's that knew with so much death. The love and affection that any women had to give was nothing no more than a blessing, they were so close but at the same time...very distance. Although they were within arm reach of each of us as I could understand why they protected these females. It was like if they were the last on this earth and

I so needed one of them to help me out with this coldness as I inquired about communication that they may have.

They seem to be more worried about ours but it had been destroyed as we could smell the burning of the forest throughout that night. We bedded down with a small fire bucket that kept us warm while one of us stayed up one by one just in case they were pirates. They was the worst type peoples as they were nothing more than slave traders among our own kind to our invaders. There was nothing surprising about this invasion anymore as I believe that I have seen it all, it was morning time as we had gotten up searching the skies for patrolling alien crafts.

It was something strange about this place that none of us could touch, it was just too peaceful with all that was going on. Everyone was so well feed and seem to be living without fear as we stayed several days in some area call the Ohio Snake River. We were surrounded by trees that limited us from travel but protected us from our invaders as we returned to our small transport aircraft that had been destroyed to nothing. Another week had gone by but several days back we had been approached without notice and ask to relinquish our weapon without warning.

We suspected so much negativity was going on, it all happen 2days after we returned from our aircraft that had been surrounded by aliens. We could see them from the way they landed until they had taking off. We knew there was nothing for them to take because our computer system had already been remove. We suspected that it was these farmers that had taking us in but it was hard to prove knowing they knew we were in the area from being shot down.

They locked us up for more than several days while giving us no choice but to escape. We took several lives while losing them as well but once we gotten back to Washington DC. We all had to give full reports of the alien activity that had been going on with that little farming area. But nothing but residue had been found as that little hidden farming town was nothing more than ashes along with several alien spaceships. All had been destroyed for whatever reason, it wasn't all for nothing. It only prove what existed even though nothing was left that could've giving us more information on their secret activities.

Chapter 13

INTERSPACE UNIVERSAL PROTECTOR

It been several years into the fighting, this world was on the brink of destruction from this madness knowing we knew that deep down. We had no way in hell of winning this war but we are too ignorant to know when we are been beat. So much pride lived in us, maybe because we were Americans and adapted to a certain way of life and wanted nothing less. Even the poor and us n*ggas expected a certain quality of living in this land of freedom.

We now suffered in more ways than we could ever imagine and our own President who brightly red hair was showing streaks of grey. Her life was nothing more than stress as our soldiers fought the death that wanted them from every direction known to us. Some areas were nothing more than death traps as they begin pushing deeper into our homes overtaking our neighborhood. Everyone human was subject to some form of death and been a drifter or farmer was like committing suicide.

You were stronger in numbers but it wasn't only the aliens we had to worry about, we also had foreign soldiers and mercenaries. There was so much anger that even the aliens that had been giving immigrant status was now even on the hunt. It was like if our borders was nothing more than penetrated and even we knew that it would only be a matter of time before they are all rounded up like cattle's. We had come across many that had been killed and beheaded for the reward they had coming to them.

Home owners done what they could to protect what they considered there's, it was madness at its best. The only thing that I gotten from this is our invading alien species had done nothing but protect its own while observing our own inner destruction. Our communication had been badly destroyed from the many foreign invading countries that wanted their own. Maybe too much was happing and more consideration should have been taking place before crazy decisions had been sent forward.

We had to find ways to keep the communication going, it had become a job within itself while often our military had been left in the dark, even with all the technology we had. But they destroyed ours with their high powered weapons and mortar attacks, we had done the same to our invading enemies. So much death was among us for the first time in our history that our Generals had to deploy troops within our own country. I fought several wars and done so many missions but if anyone would have ever told me that this was going to happen to us, it would have been none stop laughing.

But this was no laughing matter with all that was going on and even more as NASA had pick up another incoming signal heading our way. It was later on that day I found myself in another meeting listening to NASA explaining to us about in less than 24 hours, we were going to know who was coming our way. The way our President paced back and forth while asking the Generals about the war that was going on. We had the upper hand but deaths was still among our soldiers but war come with death, even a child would understand that without been told of the aftermath.

The moment we had been dismissed I found myself heading down toward the basement to sleep, my home had been destroyed to nothing. It was nothing but a waste of what was once a decent neighborhood as I had awaken up by the sound of others moving about while rushing up the stairs. What we had been told earlier wasn't true as our invading aliens arrived much earlier than what we had been told. I myself had rushed to the conference room to discover that many had sat around, we expected this but who were they appearing like ghosts in the early morning like the sunrise.

Our fighter jets had been deployed, I could only hope that they don't fires upon them and they seem to be friendlier than what was already here. It didn't take long as our alien invaders had made their way as our aircrafts pulled back allowing them to take the sky, it was the strangest thing we ever saw. Not once did either of them fire upon each other while we intercepted communications among them. It had done us no good as we couldn't understanding their language.

Maybe they were friends and if so, this would only make it harder for us to not just fight one invading force but now two. We monitored their behavior while continuing fighting our invaders, maybe they were the real alien race and what he had been fighting was there slaves or something. We never truly know due to the lack of communication with our Foreign Invaders while their destruction continued upon us worldwide. It wasn't until the 2nd day that they made their way toward our White House, they had come in peace is what we gather.

NASA played a major part as we could see them appearing from thin air outside our gates, we knew something like this would happen as they deployed many of their smaller spaceships about the area. What they done was similar to what we would have done as they secured the area before they even exit there spaceships. Our president was nothing more than fearless as she greeted them on the front lawn, I would have never expected this as I awaken this morning.

This was the most important women in the world and yet she was making her way toward this alien species as the unknown now stood before us. The way they look upon us couldn't be describe as her Secret Service Agents moved closer to her.

"Welcome to our world, im am the President Hillary of the United State and this is my Staff."

"Im Commander of the Universal Protector Interspace Federation of Galaxies

It was that moment the President reached out to greet this unknown species who stood in silence before reaching out toward her. This was one of the best sights we have ever seen before as everyone who look on cheered. Not just here but maybe around the world as both of them made their way toward a sitting area. We stood surrounding them as it seem to be inspect everything. Darken clouds had begun to appear, it was that moment, this event was taking inside as I wonder was this a good. I could hear her advisors telling her but she had the last word.

"I have to apologize for the condition of the White House, we recently just taking control of it about a few months back, you can see how it was destroyed." President Hillary said.

I really didn't think this alien cared.

"This the oval office."

Carpenters had left as they were ask as I watched our politicians find seats while somewhat coughing from the burnt smell. It was somewhat irritating.

"Madam President, your world is being destroyed as we speak and within a year time or two, it would be nothing that you want be able to recognized if you are able to live through it." Interspace Universal Protector Commander Qknya said.

"I'm aware of our situation but it didn't start out this way as they had begun to spread themselves out more and more like a disease around the world." President replied.

"We have been monitoring your world since we pick up their travel to this distance galaxy that even we didn't know existed." I.S.U.P Commander Qkunya explained.

"May I ask why are you here and why didn't they attack your spaceships, they are destroyers of the worst kind from what we gather." President said.

"We come to your world in peace and as long as we pose no threat, they cannot fire upon us, as I represent Interspace Universal Protector, we are a Federation of many Species from around the Universe as you can see before you President." I.S.U.P Commander Qkunya said.

"Ok, now why are you here?" President ask.

"I come here not to fight your war but to keep it equal." Ms. President.

"It good to hear that but as you can see, we can't match their fire power, it like they are playing with us all around the world." President said.

"What this world is experiencing is a form of unknown but this is what the Arneulians do to worlds they invade before they infest you with disease and virus while changing your genetics forever and the lucky ones will die." I.S.U.P Commander Qkunya said.

"What have we done to them and why our world?" President Hillary ask with frustration in her voice.

"We have monitored there communication data and what we come up with is that, they come to your world looking for escape slaves and wanted them back, is this correct?" I.S.U.P Commander Qkunya ask.

That moment I notice the President gotten quiet from what she just heard was true and all this could've been avoided if she just would have giving them up.

*"**What you say is true, they were slaves but after 10 years, we made them citizens.**"*

"We are not here to judge your way of thinking but your technology is so ancient that you started a war with a much aggressive Alien Species that will destroy this world and drained it to nothing." I.S.U.P Commander Qkunya responded calmly.

*"**Can you give us advice?**"*

"Madam President even if you did find a way to destroy them and pushed them from your world, you would have still done no harm to them because what you see is not even 2% of their species. I.S.U.P Commander Qkunya said.

*"**It good that you have come to our world and giving us this knowledge and if you can find a way to give us aid or help in anyway like technology." 'We will be very grateful as I don't want my world to end within death and disease when it is all said and done." President said.***

Silence came about the room as we watched this alien get up making its way toward one of his own kind who stood like a mighty soldier.

*"**Madam President we come here to make this war fair...meaning that technology has to be equal to the same and by interspace universal law, they have to fight you with what you have." I.S.U.P Commander Qkunya explained.***

"We really need your help or we are all going to die here before we know it unless your armies can help us."

*"**Madam President we can't aide you in that way as I said before but what we can do can change your entire way of life." I.S.U.P Commander Qkunya responded.***

"Our own citizens live in fear, some fight back but overall, they are been control by our invaders and the only hope they seem to have is death." President Hillary explained.

*"**What we can offer you is technology to defend your world." I.S.U.P Commander Qkunya responded.***

"How is this possible and when will it happen?"

"Madam President what we have to offer, can't just be giving this nation but the entire world." I.S.U.P Commander Qkunya replied.

"Why, we are the big brother to this world and if this technology is to change our world, it must be kept among this country!" President said somewhat loudly.

It was that moment of her raising her voice had brought nothing but silence among the alien protectors as they stared at each other. We could hear them bickering among themselves before turning back toward us.

"Madam President if we only give this country this vast technology, we wonder what you would do with this technology long after we have left your world." 'We know of your history from beginning to end and with this being you have call God and he sent his son Jesus to repeat your sins to a better after life as we read this thing your world call the Holly Bible." I.S.U.P Commander Qkunya said.

He had been cut off as the President intervene explaining what this country would be like, if such technology gotten into the wrong hands like powerful foreign enemy aggressors.

"Madam President your entire species fight with each other over land and whatever you deem to have value as we fear that this technology would only place your existence on a higher level of control and beyond this world as well." 'We fear that you will invade other peaceful planets beyond this one and that that you may spread death that you are born to give from birth." I.S.U.P Commander Qkunya said.

"Our culture maybe as you say but overall, we all just want to live in peace while protecting our own and evil is taught from birth."

"Madam President your entire world history is like the sight you are giving, this maybe our biggest regret as we give you this technology to not just protect what you believe in but it will allow you to travel with the stars." 'This is why you must bring all your world leader together, so this maybe giving to all at once." I.S.U.P Commander Qkunya said.

"So much has happen within our world that what you ask maybe impossible right now, even more so at this time."

"Madam President your world is on the brink of destruction and if you fail to provide me with this simple request, all that you

know will be nothing more than a memory." 'Desperate times call for desperate measures as your world says." I.S.U.P Commander Qkunya said calmly.

"How much time do you need to make this happen?"

"Madam President the longer you take, the more lives you will lose daily, you don't have long before the Arneulians ends all you have known and force you into slavery without remorse because this is what they do." *'This world is so young and full of life, they will flourish within this small planet and reap its wealth of the land and oceans has to offer." I.S.U.P Commander Qkunya said calmly.*

"These, Arneulians has destroyed the majority of our Navy and Submarines to almost nothing, we still have some capability to reproduce but with their aggressive attacks without notice" 'As much as I hate to bring such words as spies among us, they do exist, we know it want be long before some of our capability is lost forever."

"Madam President we are aware of your losses and the destruction that you have face in not just your own country but this entire world is facing a life ending crisis that is spreading like an uncontrollable virus that can't be contain." *'We are here to help and share this technology among your world that may prevent your species as a whole" 'What we can do is bring your scientist and engineers and with our technology, we can give you the information you need to know, this technology will provide you with everything you need to know to defend your world as one." 'You must all come together to push them from your existence or you may fail as a whole." I.S.U.P Commander Qkunya explained.*

"Madam President that you are telling me is that you will bring us aboard your spaceship and give us all this life changing technology."

We continue to listen as he spoke of our nuclear weapons that just doesn't destroy one country that it's aimed at but the world in general. We could all tell from his expression that he wasn't satisfied from the destruction that we could bring on ourselves. This day was coming to an end but with everything on the line.

Chapter 14

"RUNAI"

It didn't give us much time because for month to month of negotiation, all I knew as that we were been exterminated daily and there wasn't much we could do but continue the fight the best we could knowing by the end of the day. We lost the battles no matter where we were in this world, but I can never forget the hard fighting battles that we found victory in as well. It had only taking us a week time before we had come together while putting our conflict aside for right now.

There was so many world leaders from the smallest country to the biggest super powers, it wasn't like we had much choice right now. This technology that we were able to experience was vaster than anything we could even imagine. The conference room that we had all been brought into was nothing more that amazing from technology that we never seen from the closing of the doors to the simple seating that appeared from thin air.

The food that had been offered seem to give us life, it alone would have been worth billions in our culture, as I look around. I bet no one in their life would have ever seen this coming and that was with our newly visitors that we made a part of our world with time. With so many alien species that we never seen before walking about catering to our every need, we truly aren't alone in this world, our only problem was that we didn't have the technology to reach out to them. But as we now see and understand this unknown mystery that they did know of us all this time.

We applauded their respect for us but it wasn't all love and war, some of them seem to have no respect for what we stood for or what we are it seems. I understood in many ways as a black man because America has treated us like invaders but we never invaded nothing from the beginning. My first breath only meant negativity and for sure resentment only because my skin is darker than those of the celebrated birth in this land of the free, the red…the white…the blue. As we all watch this alien approached.

"Welcome, nations of earth, my name is Runai and I am an Interspace Universal Protector Engineer, it will be my job to make sure that you scientists and engineers and scholars learned this technology that may save your world." Runai spoke loudly.

So much hate filled this room but it wasn't for the aliens but us in general but with years of war and devastation, it was easy to see how. This event was nothing more than a joke, it took longer to make the simplest decision than it did for the transportation. I guess it wasn't for nothing as we gathers our smartest from round the world. I was lucky to be one of the chosen ones that was allowed to witness this unbelievable process. Yet we still had so much going on from the small battles to our own soldiers simply just deserting to search for their families.

Many was prosecuted but with the overcrowding of prisons, it was easier to put a bullet in their head but even that became inhumane with so much negativity going on. It had become easier to give them what they needed and released them. At least this way, they were still able to fight on our side, this had become our reality but we were facing a new disease that we had no cure for. Our smartest in the world was being transformed into human computers with information that was hundreds of years before our time.

I myself had witness some had taking on so much information that the impossible had become possible. Some had developed the powers to move objects without touch alone with mind control of others. Some with once calm personalities had become aggressive and uncontrollable rage and yet some even died from becoming too smart. It wasn't a bad thing because we needed to rid out the weak while the strong continue to progress in ways that they would become a forever threat to our world. Even I knew that such individuals would be monitored until there death as I knew when I retired from government service.

This knowledge was giving in increments, it was the only safe way, our minds was amazing but with each death taking place. We learned from the last. Once the powerful countries departed 3 Mothership, the other had begun the process. Phase two of this process wasn't going to be easy but we had no choice but to push forward as we did. In the process we lost several transformation areas due to we didn't have the means too completely fight off their air attacks. Our ground forces fought like if their lives depended on it and with time, they will be all rewarded for what they done before their deaths.

It was nothing but a sight to see, it was unbelievable to even begin with as we transformed what had been considered rust bucket into flying fortress. These old antique battleships was now ready for war and we even brought in what was left of an aging veteran fighting force back into service. These old tymers was proud to be back in service fighting for their country alone with the younger generation that could've been there grandson son and daughters easily. This war had been change as our gun blazed from above and missiles fired upon our Alien Invaders as they had been doing us for the last several years.

Our airplanes that once sat under the burning Tucson sun and other storage facilities was now back in operation. With so many upgrades has turn these once fossils dinosaurs into high tech fighting machines that was able to destroy our invaders. It didn't take long before this was happening all around the world as we had become one. We were now a complete fighting unit and with high tech voice recognition systems, our communication had become our greatest weapon with this life changing technology.

For the next few years blood stained our world, there was times that it seem that this was never going to end, especially with our hospitals. Death was rolling out just as fast as bodies was entering them, anything that could shelter had become medical wards. So many peoples around the world done what they could for the sick injured and dying. This was our revelation on earth it seem and I witness so much of it firsthand.

Our once most feared problem of racism and economical divide between the rich and poor didn't mean much anymore. It didn't matter which crotch you were snatch out of, American had no choice but to put their difference aside and come together and unite as one because we had enough to deal with. Local criminals were often released from jails as the towns and city begin to fail. Life sentences was still a problems but the federal government wasn't as lenient and the only answer they had come up with was immediately death.

I could imagine been fired upon while still in your cell cage like an animal, maybe that was the easy way to die if they could afford the bullet. The thought of them coming up with ways to killed you inexpensively and cheap. Our country of civilized laws didn't even give you the opportunity of trail and jury in some parts of beloved red white and blue. With so much death coming from all directions and neighborhoods becoming small communities.

Most judges had either became the elder man or woman or anyone who took it upon themselves to keep some kind of peace among the laws that still existed. This had become crazy times and the hardship of living wasn't getting better by the next coming day. In fact with so much destruction, crimes was growing for mere survival and nothing was safe. Not even the bolts in the ground if they were needed for something, there wasn't much innocence anymore among us. I myself like to think that it was just us Americans who had being giving everything from birth in this once land of plenty.

But even I knew that wasn't true, these Invading Aliens was like an airborne disease that had the capability to cross mighty storming oceans without any kind of fear. But somehow the God giving sun had broken through the stench of a lion ass. It was Christmas day that would never be the same for us from this day on. Only because this was the day that we realized that the war that we had been fighting ended.

The day of giving had turned out to become the day of independence once again from the invaders that made their way into world placing fear worldwide. We force them from our world but we lost a large part of our population in the process changing not just America but the world as we know it. We rebuilt so much that had been destroyed but we face a new problems with our new births. Our, DNA had been infected worldwide from our invaders and now we were to live with the result of there once presence.

Our world suffered heavily from life killing bacteria's to unknown diseases that we had no cure and the death you wanted often didn't come the second you wanted it. We continue to search the oceans and great lakes for the remainder of there under water cities that nearly destroyed our Navy and Coast Guard. So many ships had being sunken that now lay at the bottom or depths that we can't even imagine getting to but I guess that what happen in war.

Chapter 15

"THE WHITE HOUSE"

Several years has now past and it was time to get our political system back on track, it was decided by unanimous decision by Congress that our President remain in power. So much destruction upon our world caused by our Foreign Invaders only made it an easy decision especially due to our population living in despair. But now the Republicans party wanted a shot at the title but I personally felt that our Commander in Chief has seen enough. You could look in her eyes and tell that she wasn't going to run for re-election and it was time for her to find some peace in what was left of her insanity.

This is what I truly felt since I spent the majority of my time by her side and even more behind closed doors as I take notice of another Christmas approaching. We celebrated their departure like clockwork as it was nothing but an honor to have work with her. It wasn't long after, I had been invited back to the White House for what reason, I had no idea. The only reason for me being there was the protection of our alien guest and eventually I became her aid during our Earth Invasion.

But with that being said, neither one really existed anymore but I had address the invitation and made my way there a week later. I remember that day I enter alone with many politicians from senators to congressman and here I was a no body among men's of honor. I sat there after the long process of just getting through the door, it was like if no one was to be trusted. Maybe it was because so many spies that help our Alien Invaders during the war was still among us.

We had all sat patiently while I listens to one to many political conversations about what should be done to rebuild this country. There was nothing I could say but we all gotten suspicious to what this was about when we saw U.S Marines escorting Interspace Universal Protectors. The moment everyone had taking seats while the President entered before we all sat around the round table.

"Welcome everyone, this is a meeting of concern from our guest as you see, each of you were especially invited for numerous reasons and I want each of you to give full attention and respect to our I.S.U.P's here." President Hillary said.

"The reason I come here concern is not just for this world but the universe as I speak, and with this concern, we have many questions." I.S.U.P Commander Qkunya said.

It was that moment that everyone gotten quiet as they just looked at each other.

"Please explain to me what you are talking about because, im sure that I'm not the only one that has concern about what you are saying, so if you can." 'Please explain a little more directly about what you are saying commander Qkunya" President said.

We all sat waiting to see what he was going to say.

"This world has endured so much within the last few years from devastation hardship to life ending of your world but you survive with the technology that we gave you." I.S.U.P Commander Qkunya said.

Before he could continue talking, she had cut him off aggressively.

"Commander, we are very grateful for what you have done and it's been numerous years now that you have been a part of our world monitoring us like children's, you are aware that we can take care of ourselves." President said somewhat aggressive loudly.

"We are no threat to you or your planets but with all that has happen, this has become my assignment to monitors and report any suspicious activity to the Interspace Council Association of the Universe." 'What I represent is just a mere dot of my organization as I have explained before Madam President." I.S.U.P Commander Qkunya repeated calmly.

"I understand and respect your position of authority but we are now a rebuilding world of what was destroyed by an Invading Notorious Hostile Alien Species." President Hilary said.

"*We are here not just to protect your world from destruction but to also monitor for the Planetary of Federation that exist far beyond this tiny galaxy of unlivable planets.*" *I.S.U.P Commander Qkunya explained.*

"**If we are what you say, than how can this tiny little area be such a universal threat?**" **President Hillary ask.**

No one said nothing in response as they looked puzzle because each of them knew of earthly greed and power of dominance alone with lies and betrayal to get what they want. Maybe for a brief moment, they thought of themselves and what they had done to achieve what they wanted. It was all I could come up with as I glanced around the room looking at their facial features that hide who they really were maybe.

"**You know Commander Qkunya you can leave our world anytime you feel free.**" **President Hillary said.**

It was that moment that he look toward his Staff who said nothing but done as they were told as we look on noticing what they were doing. It was no bigger than a sandwich holder but it displayed our entire world to a micro science before our face. We saw nothing more than fascination before our very eyes, we had been giving so much technology but we was far from everything they never shown us. The way he moved his hand among this visual displayed that didn't required a wall, but blended in the air. I can't even describe what I was looking at to be honest.

"**This is your world and the flashing light are radioactive signal that we have detected, what is strange about these signal are none of them are coming from your reactors.**" **I.S.U.P Commander Qkunya explained.**

"*Commander, what you are looking at is nothing more than radioactive hotspot from within the earth from its core.*" *President Hillary responded.*

The room had become completely silence as they seem to know what he was talking about but I didn't have a clue.

"**These radioactive signal are interspace transference radio waves, nothing about this has to do with your earth core but it does have a lot to do with your earth gravitational field alone with the technology that we giving you.**" **I.S.U.P Commander Qkunya stated mildly.**

Once again everyone look around in silence.

"**Commander Qkunya, I really have no idea of what you are taking about but I will get with my scientist and engineers to get to the bottom of this.**" **President Hillary said.**

Once again the room gotten quiet as we listening to him instruct his Staff once more to bring up documentation of his version of proof.

"Madam President, you are the most powerful woman in the world and it is you that I will work with, if you look toward the hologram once again." 'I like to show you of many locations around the world that we have been picking variation of radioactive material similar to the technology that we giving you to transform your battleship from earth gravitational field." I.S.U.P Commander Qkunya explained calmly again.

I watched the President come to her feet's and walk around looking at the ISUP's saying nothing for a minute.

"You are nothing no more than a spy reporting back to whomever right!" President Hillary yelled.

"We are Interspace Universals Pro,"

It was that moment the President had cut him off saying how she has heard it more than a hundred times about who and what you are. We all watched her blow her top and not once did anyone of them interfere as they continue to let her get louder. It was easy to understand why she was getting out of control, this is a woman who had the world on her shoulder and never had the chance to breaks down or even cry.

"Your emotion and anger has been your enemy from the beginning of your existence upon this world that you were brought to." I.S.U.P Commander Qkunya said.

"What do you mean by that?" President Hillary ask loudly.

"What I said must be disregarded for the protection of your religious belief alone with who and what you believe that you are Madam President." I.S.U.P Commander Qkunya said.

It was that moment she just look at him alone with everyone been fascinated about what has just came from his mouth.

"You have to tell me what you just said under you Federation Hand Book of Interspace Regulatory Alliance." 'Admiral…Do you have a downloaded copy on that computer system?" President Hillary ask.

"Yes Madam President." Admiral Thornton responded quickly.

"Get it, I need to show it to our good Commander Qkunya here." President Hillary ask.

We watched him instruct his Lieutenant to do what had just been ask.

"There is no need for that Madam President, im aware of our handbook and it rules and regulation." I.S.U.P Commander Qkunya said.

This room had gotten so quiet that we could hear each other breathing until he leaned forward in his seat getting ready to talk.

"You were once a species of difference far from a galaxy that was destroyed by your own who branched off to nearby planets." 'The destruction that you brought to yourself along with the species that you conquered and turn them into slaves and with time the weapons you created destroyed each other." 'Our job is to protect the universe from annulation or prevent death of an entire species if possible." 'With so much destruction upon what you were, it was voted that we remove what was left of the planets you destroyed and bring you to one that was so far from anyone, preventing this from ever happening again." 'You humans have great ability from birth but you also have an inner ability to rule to conquer and rule by nature and that make you a universal threat alone to civilized galaxies." 'You are the third planet from the sun and it was here that you started from scratch and we would have never thought you would progress again the way you are." 'But with time you did and it was voted to let your invaders destroy you with time but it must be on an equal playing field." 'What I represent save your existence before, it was decided by the Planetary of Federation to do it again." I.S.U.P Commander Qkunya explained.

Not a word had been said as the President couldn't believe what she was hearing as we were all puzzled and very hard to imagine that we existed before in this world.

"You are telling me that we was once mighty warriors and we branched way from each other only to destroy each other?" President Hillary ask.

"Yes Madam President, you human are your own destroyers and yes you were universal rulers, this technology we gave you was maybe the biggest mistake ever but now you have it." 'So I ask you Madam President…is this world transforming their vessels to universal space travel?" 'We also believe that you are preparing for a massive invasion to your Invaders and if this is

what you are doing, you will only destroy what you are as a whole." I.S.U.P Commander Qkunya said mildly.

"What you done for us wasn't a mistake but it only made us stronger as we now has enhance this technology even more." *'You have giving us the means to protect our world and live in peace with each other now that we know how it feels to be almost destroyed altogether."* **President Hillary said.**

"Madam President, it would be nice if you could just answer my questions so we may decide what to do with the information giving." I.S.U.P Commander Qkunya asked.

"Our world was invaded and almost destroyed only because we had taking in this Alien Species who they said was there slaves." *'We sat down with them in a civilized manner and done our best to keep this from happen."* *'Where were you at then, were you monitoring that?"* **President Hillary ask.**

Not one of them responded, it was nothing but silence among them.

"Are we to be cowards, did you know that for the 3 years they invaded us, they left their seeds behind all over the world and yet we are still finding their offspring that are hard to detect accept when we test the babies and now little children." *'Are you aware that there growth changes without notice according to our doctors and what going to happen when these seeds pushing into our society, maybe even become part of our political world?"* *'And why did they all leave at once so easy when we were on the verge of destruction?"* **President Hillary ask aggressively.**

"You have discovered time warp capability and we have monitored your vessels leaving your own galaxy and returning, why is this?" I.S.U.P Commander Qkunya ask.

Silence had come amongst everyone.

"Whatever this world is attempting to do like going past this little galaxy, we cannot let you travel beyond your existence into another in search of war or even to explore." I.S.U.P Commander Qkunya said.

"We are not bound by your laws nor are we limited from exploration from our galaxy and if we are?" *'Please explain to us even more as we have downloaded all that you stand for." President Hillary said.*

Silence had come among everyone.

"Your technology has advance faster than we could ever assumed but with technology also come responsibility and we fear that you are not ready for what is beyond this small dead galaxy." I.S.U.P Commander Qkunya said.

"You have no idea of what we are capable of or our strength and we are the creation of God who sent his son into this world to forgive us for our sins." President Hillary explained.

I.S.U.P Commander Qkunya had done nothing but sat there and listen, we could only imagine what he thought when he just explained to us, who and what we are before we existed on earth. I could only imagine what the world would think if they heard the same story about our existence, religion has played a major part of our lives since birth and to tell us that God wasn't our creator alone with everything you claim he has done for us. It alone made me wonder if there really is a heaven or hell after hearing what had just been said.

Chapter 16

"Invasion Aftermath"

It has now been three years of preparation from so many countries around the world that wanted to be a part of this massive invasion. We sent our political leaders all over the world recruiting countries involvement, some had been giving offers they couldn't refuse. So many was going to play major parts in this and if not, maybe it would be understood. We have all suffered from the loss of loved ones to families completely destroyed along with their homes and everything they ever work for.

It was nothing but destruction of so many tears, it had become better to see something you love and ashes burned down to nothing. Then for it to be still standing and unlivable, nothing about this invasion have produce any form of positivity. We had gotten to appoint, that finding qualified personnel had become even a tasks for a country that was greater than most. But with so much in the past of death and destruction, it alone had change people's mentality. Especially those who done everything by the book.

But even I knew when you are force to see your family starve or even be taken by aliens and the sad part is that. Even you know, there was nothing you could do to stop what has been done and being a one man army or overnight hero only resulted in your death. Not to mention how you put yourself in a situation to be taken as well. It must be the craziest feeling to have inside knowing there is a strong chance that you may never return.

That kind of devastation can leave you without a return home, just as we emptied out our prisons so did many other countries, causing a strange domino effect within this madness. All eyes were still on America, it was never an easy task to get inmates to act like well-disciplined soldiers. Because in reality, they were not and was so much anger and frustration built inside of them from our prison systems and unfair justice system. It had become a major problem for us trying to transform them into what we want them to become.

The thought alone of them being force into a system that had taken away their freedom for the crimes they committed and yet, some of them still claims their innocence. I myself can never say it was a bad thing because some of them accepted the false hopes from a government that offered once them the key to the cities once they return home. But even I knew that wasn't true as I watched them being fitted with electrical monitoring devices and some was even fitted with decapitation collars. It was unbelievable to see but I guess it was needed if something went wrong or they turned on us.

It was simply designed to decapitate them on the spot causing rapid blood loss. Some was even injected with tiny capsules designed to release deadly poison. Nothing about this was morally correct because when it was all said and done, the inmates was still a person with feeling and family who loved them somewhere. But I can understand the decisions that have been made, because in so many ways our backs was up against the wall and we had no choice but to push for and fight back.

The death that was facing wasn't just an individual now, it was us as a nation knowing we didn't have many choices right now. It wasn't all thrown out to the dogs, some of these inmates fought like warriors while dying like harden Battlefield Soldiers. We gave them the same honor as we did our uniform soldiers, some say we treated them like if they didn't even exist. Some even believe that white's inmates wasn't giving suicide mission, in my eyes it was true but who was I to bring change. These men's stood before their Commanders as I watched those received awards in this time of honor and death.

It was nothing but an amazing beautiful sight to see, what was consider outcast now facing their biggest transformation alone with what comes from bravery at its best. So amazing to be a part of but the one that I had become fond of was this Lt. Colonel who had been decorated by the President herself. This man have been given the rank of full bird along with the Medal of Honor. This was the same officer that only a few years ago that she wanted him stripped of his entire command and demoted to nothing in rank.

We had all been call to attention, we stood proudly like if we were graduating Boot Camp. Secretary of Defense Allison had been brought in on this one as he spoke highly for what had been done. We all had taken notice of the President tears knowing she remembered that day like yesterday. Secretary of Defense Allison spoke of the bravery that had been done that day near the Canadian Border.

I don't want to get into a long story but it would be hard from what was been said of the Presidential plane on their way back. It had been sent from an attack, it was as if the aliens knew of their flight plan from their awaiting ground force. So much had been done from the way Air Force One escorting planes had been taken out without notice. Spies had to be involve, such betrayal was nothing more than ignorance but nothing wasn't far from the truth of this reality that we are facing.

So many believe that we were better off once our invaders take control of our world for the loyalty giving but once the Air Force One sent out an emergency signal. No one was insight to come to her aide but somehow Lt. Colonial moved his force toward the border. That when he notice Patrolling Alien Crafts. What should have been negativity was nothing more than a blessing. He was about 15 minutes from his assigned area but because he was nothing more than a rebel, his Commander in Chief.

President herself escape pod would not have never been protected from the fierce battle between the Aliens and his Fighting Force. Many more awards had been handed out but he was the only one to have the Medal of Honor placed around his neck. He had also receive the rank of full Colonel in front of the remainder of his team. He also presented his lost soldiers awards to their families because many died protecting the President life.

This was nothing more than a tearjerker for everyone who looked on, the media ate it up like fresh hot cakes smoother in hot maple syrup. I wondered if she thought about that day that she when she wanted to demoted him to nothing, it's amazing how life work itself out sometime. I personally believe that his entire existence was meant for that one moment, maybe his act of bravery brought great change that we are yet to see. I now live in her shadow but I truly believe that if the aliens would have gotten a hold her as they intended to.

We may be facing an entire different way of living only because I believe that deep inside her was nothing but a scared little girl with her big mouth. Knowing I could never say that to her or make certain comment in public regarding what I thought. Such word would not be a good outcome and my life maybe greatly affected in the worst way knowing we were fighting an Alien Species. They were fierce not just in battle but their way of living and with so much negativity between us and them, we often came across alien survivors.

They would cut out their own tongue before giving us any information that we could use against them. We giving them food but not one consume it as we watch them starve before our face with food by their side.

We so wanted to hate them but we could do nothing but admire their dedication. They were true warriors and often took their own life by crashing into our structure knowing they were bringing death upon themselves.

I can't degrade our own because we fought just as hard from one day to the next even though we know, that death was within a blink of an eye. Each day we lost by large numbers and no matter what we said before sending our man's off to fight. At the end of the day, many graves had been dug, some even buried their own buddies and it had gotten to appoint that gun stores gave weapons to anyone who was willing and able. Money didn't mean nothing to basic survival, homeless wasn't look down upon because anything treasure could be taking without warning.

These invaders came like the mist been sprayed from an aerosol can and vanishing just as quickly. Americans were being exterminated but the world knew that this death would pushed beyond our borders with time. It was long after, our own technology was been turned against us but we never gave up from beginning to end. I remember how it was just 10 years ago when I discovered these helpless starving aliens who invaded my rusty old camper for food.

I wonder what would of happen if the government didn't intervene and give them citizenship. Even though their freedom was limited but with time, some fought these invaders but now it was time for others to step up. Their knowledge should play a major role if victory is coming our way especially having numerous species. We knew that each one had their own special ability, there were no magical powers but each of their species were unique. But with time, our scientist had come up with new ways of using our own nuclear weapons but the way we were been watch. Arneulians didn't have much to worry about due to the Interspace Universal Protectors.

The most feared of them all were the Blacken because they had the ability to read your inner thoughts. This was the main reason why they were kept malnourished every way possible but America didn't allow slavery. It didn't take much to convince them to see it our way but even with that, we were told of the fear that Blacken could give us. With time we had come to see why this species was very dangerous, it alone made them untrustworthy.

Even more so if they were not in your presence, their knowledge of an individual history from birth, not to mention your intentions. Brilliance at his best knowing that ability made them truly amazing and with time. We done everything we could to learn of their existence while enhancing our own ability to a point that we even made clones of them. Several years passed and our political system was down falling, Congress had come up with a unanimous decision that our President remain in power.

So much destruction our Foreign Invaders brought upon us leaving us in despair, but with time the Republicans party wanted a shot at the title. I personally felt that our Commander in Chief has seen enough. Her expression shown it and my belief is that she should step down and search for some kind of inner peace of what was left of her insanity. Not long after another Christmas was approaching it was nothing but an honor to work by her side.

Not long after I found myself back in the White House remembering that day I enter. So many politicians and here I was a no body among men's of power as I taken my seat knowing with all that was going on. We had alien spies and no one was to be trusted as I sat patiently listens to one to many political conversations about what should be done regarding this country. The sight of Marines escorting Interspace Universal Protectors open our eyes widely as we watch them take their seats.

That moment only seconds later, our President walk in.

"Welcome everyone, this is a meeting of concern from our guest as you see, each of you were especially invited for numerous reasons and I want each of you to give full attention and respect to our ISUP's here."

"Madam President the reason I come here concern is not just for this world but the universe as I speak, and with this concern, we have many questions." I.S.U.P Commander said.

It was that moment everyone gotten quiet as they just looked at each other.

"Please explain to me what you are talking about because, im sure that I'm not the only one that has concern about what you are saying, so if you can." 'Please explain a little more directly about what you are saying because if we are what you say." 'Than how can this tiny little area be such a universal threat Commander?"

"Madam President it not what you are but what you have the capability to become and if not you, than another within this world that poses a threat beyond this existence." I.S.U.P Commander Qkunya said.

No one said nothing in response while looking puzzle because each of them knew of earthly greed and power of dominance alone with lies and betrayal to get what they want. Maybe for a brief moment, they thought of themselves and what they had done to achieve what they wanted. It's all I could come up with while glancing around the room looking facial features that maybe was hiding who they really were.

"You know Commander Qkunya…you can leave our world anytime you feel free." President Hillary said.

It was that moment the President had cut him off saying how she heard it more than a hundred times about who and what you are. We watched her blow her top and not once did anyone of them interfere as they continue to let her get louder. It was easy to understand why she was getting out of control, this is a woman who had the world on her shoulders and never had the chance to breaks down or even cry.

"Your emotion and anger has been your enemy from the beginning of your existence upon this world that you were brought to."

"What do you mean by that Commander Qkunya?"

"Madam President what I said must be disregarded for the protection of your religious belief alone with who and what you believe that you are Madam President."

It was that moment everyone look at *Commander Qkunya* with fascination about what came from his mouth.

"You have to tell me what you just said under your Federation Hand Book of Interspace Regulatory Alliance."

"It better that nothing is said from this point on what I just spoke President Hillary." Commander Qkunya said.

"Admiral...do you have a downloaded copy on that computer system of your?"

"Yes Madam President." Admiral Thornton responded quickly.

"Get it, I need to show it to our good Commander Qkunya here." **President said.**

We watched him instruct his Lieutenant do what had just been ask from his computer system that sat on the table before him.

"There is no need for that Madam President, im aware of our handbook and it rules and regulations." I.S.U.P Commander Qkunya said.

This room had gotten so quiet that we could hear each other breathing until he leaned forward in his seat getting ready to talk.

"You were once a species of difference far from a galaxy that was destroyed by your own who branched off to nearby planets." 'The destruction that you brought to yourself along with the species that you conquered and turned them into slaves and with time the weapons you created destroyed each other." 'Our job is to protect the universe from annulation or prevent death of an entire species if possible." 'With so much destruction upon what you were, it was voted that we remove what was left of your species entirely and brought you to one that was so far from civilized galaxies." 'It was the only way to prevent this from ever happening again." 'You humans have great ability from birth but you also have an inner ability to rule to conquer by your nature alone and that make you a universal threat to all around you." 'We brought you to the planet we call Ocean and it was here, the third planet from the sun." 'This was the voted area that you were to start all over from nothing and thought you would never progress again to be what you once were." 'But with time you did as we watch you involve from nothing more that dirt." 'It was voted to let your invaders destroy you with time but our regulations as written in your handbook that it has

to be on equal playing field." 'What I represent save you before, it was decided to do it again." I.S.U.P Commander Qkunya explained.

Not a word had been said knowing the President couldn't believe what she was hearing as we were all puzzled and very hard to imagine that we existed before in this world.

"You are telling me that we was once mighty warriors and we branched way from each other only to destroy each other?"

"Yes, Madam President, you human are your own destroyers and yes you were universal rulers, this technology we gave you was maybe the biggest mistake ever but now you have it." 'So I ask you Madam if this world transforming their vessels to universal space travel?" 'We also believe that you are preparing for a massive invasion to your invaders and if this is what you are doing, you will only destroy what you are as a whole."

"Commander Qkunya what you done for us wasn't a mistake but it only made us stronger as we now has enhance this technology even more." 'You have giving us the means to protect our world and live in peace with each other now but we also know how it feels to be almost destroyed altogether."

"Madam President, it would be nice if you could just answer my questions so we may decide what to do with the information giving."

"Commander Qkunya our world was invaded and almost destroyed only because we had taking in this Alien Species who they said was there slaves." 'We sat down with them in a in a civilized manner and done our best to keep this from happen." 'Where were you then, were you monitoring that?"

Not one of them responded, it was nothing but silence among them.

"Are we to be cowards, did you know that for the 3 years they invaded us, they left their seeds behind all over the world and yet we are still finding their offspring that are hard to detect accept when we test the babies and little children's." 'Are you aware that there growth changes without notice according to our doctors and what going to happen when these little demon seeds pushing into our society, maybe even become part of our political world?" 'And why did they all leave at once so easy when we were on the verge of their destruction?"

"President Hillary you have discovered time warp capability and we have monitored your vessels leaving your own galaxy and returning, why is this?"

"Commander Qkunya what're you talking about?"

Silence had come among us, we could see how these Universal Protectors didn't was lacking patients now.

"Madam President whatever this world is attempting to do like going past this little dead galaxy, we cannot let you travel beyond your existence into another."

"Commander Qkunya we are not bound by your laws nor are we limited from exploration from our so call dead galaxy and if we are, please explain to us even more as we have downloaded all that you stand for."

"Madam President you are bound by our laws and regulations when you agreed to accept our technology.

Silence had come among everyone once again as they sat there looking at each other as if they were talking with their body language and facial expression and minor sounds. As the General made a commit about so much movement going on between them.

"Madam President your technology has advance faster than we could ever assumed but with technology also come responsibility and we fear that you are not ready for what is beyond this small galaxy."

"Commander Qkunya you have no idea of what we are capable of or our strength and we are the creation of God who sent his son into this world to forgive us for our sins." President Hillary explained.

I.S.U.P Commander Qkunya had done nothing but sat there and listen, we could only imagine what he thought when he just explained to us, who and what we are before we existed on earth. I could only imagine what the world would think if they heard the same story about our existence, religion has played a major part of our lives since birth and to tell us that God wasn't our creator alone with he has done for us. It made me wonder if there really is a heaven or hell.

"You have your opinion and we have ours and who are you to tell is what we can and can't do."

"Madam President this is not up for debate on what you can and cannot do and if we have to stay around and monitor this entire tiny little planet." 'It will not be hard for us to do."

"Commander Qkunya im sure that there is no need for that and you are now free to leave our tiny little galaxy this moment as I see

that there is no other reasons for you to be within our space anymore from this point on."

"Madam President…then we have your word that you will call a stop your flights of exploration within your galaxy as I give you my word that you are no longer in danger or this world as a whole."

"Listen here Commander Qkunya, I can't stop our exploration past our world as we travel to the moon before the technology that you gave us." *'But with that been said, once again we thank you for all you have done but exploration is what we are and we will continue to explore what is around us today and tomorrow as long as we exist and once again we don't fall under any of your treaty and until we do, we will do as we please Commander!"*

"Madam President you are forbidden exploration is the orders I have receive and it is my job to enforce them for the protection of the entire galaxy."

"Commander Qkunya I see that this conversation is getting us nowhere but we are going to continue exploration as I can't control other nations but this is who and what we are!"

"Madam President as you speak, this meeting is adjourn and on behalf of what I represent, you wish is respected but you are still forbidden exploration and we are now leaving back to our home spaceship."

Chapter 17

∞∞∞

"The Count Down"

∞∞∞

We were 90 days from this massive invasion knowing I may never see home again and America was on the one yard line. This was history in the making while being on the highest alert and no one was to be trusted, we were all under watchful eyes. Suspicious activity of any kind could cause anyone to be simply rounded up like cattle and question but often resulting in immediate death 99.9% of time. So many individuals had been taken from their homes without warning of any kind.

Even I knew that many was innocent of being alien spies before death met them from the worst torture possible. So many screams I heard, it was like we were becoming uncivilized almost barbaric. Sometimes days of horror turned into weeks knowing deep inside that all the rumors of government disappearance, could become you. Death was the best medication given to cure you of the pain or mental illness of insanity that became you.

Most people's taken found ways of committing suicide, the horror of the many stories that floated about like the wind. It alone was a reason to seek death even more so if your name appeared on some government secret list of helping our invaders. Even our enemies paid for valuable information concerning America. Our destructive legal system often brought so much negativity involving our written laws and lawyers.

Defending yourself had become costly almost impossible to prove your innocence and anything concerning our invaders. Most attorneys didn't touch cases of such due to affiliation of possible guilt but with so much happening. Loyalty was becoming more important than money on any given day as our technology were becoming stronger. But with that being said, so did us being under watchful eyes as they hovered high above our Pacific Ocean and Atlantic.

It didn't take long before our notorious invaders made their way beyond our oceans into more European and Asian Countries. Our skies was constant been patrolled while our streets wasn't a stranger to their patrolling presence. We now lived a diverse lifestyle causing us so many unprofection, it didn't take long before I was looking at 60 days countdown. But it was the last 25 when my phone rang knowing it was concerning our countdown.

Wasn't long after I found myself heading back to the White House knowing it was another day of debating arguing. Maybe this was going to be our last meeting held and with everyone wanting answers knowing our problems was yet to com. Our floating spies who all seem to have serious bug living up each of their ass. Their lack of sleep and advance monitoring technology kept us on our toes.

Remembering how everyone laughed out loudly when I ask if our shit from our asses was been studied but the Universal Protectors didn't find it very funny. I arrived, my entry was long knowing no one was to be trusted. My escort also involve the Universal Protectors, it was fascinating maybe there presence was a glimpse of our future to come. We waited more than 30 minutes before the President made her way into this national conference. Security was at its highest, there patrolling was none stop as we all stood up.

"Be seated." President ordered.

We all sat back down the moment she had taking a seat while her presence was being addressed as the Universal Protectors sat in silence.

"Good afternoon once again." I.S.U.P. Commander Qkunya said.

He had taking the time to speak, we sat around waiting to see the outcome of another meeting from them.

"Madam President, our communication teams has discovered a hidden code in your computer system and this one really has our concern."

"What now Commander Qkunya, you call this meeting of United Nations to come here because you discovered a hidden code, what type of code?"

"Why're we here and what does this have to do with our country?" **German General Gerolzhoten ask.**

"Madam President this is a concern of each of you here, please look at the hologram display and even more at the location of special interest because that same code that was detected in the America NASA computer mainframe was all connected with your countries as well."

I.S.U.P Commander Qkunya explained.

"Commander Qkunya so what've you discovered if you don't mind sharing it with us?"

"Madam President if you look at the holographic diagram, you seen nothing but numbers but when I type in the transformation codes, it come up with these humanoid images." 'It puzzled us until we studied it more and this is what our computers had come up with, if you look closer." 'These images are nothing more that Arneulians clones and we have computed them by the thousands in many of your countries." 'Now why would you be manufacturing Arneulians around your world unless you were going to invade there planet?"

We watch Commander Qkunya stand there looking down on the President and then everyone else when she didn't respond with the answers he wanted to hear.

"Madam President what your world is doing is forbidden according to our handbook and if you are to invade." 'This would bring them to a very much disadvantage and just as we done to your world, we will be force to do the same to them as well." 'With that being said…we ask each of you to destroy these clowns and end whatever mission you have planned."

"Commander Qkunya explained."

"Commander Qkunya, only months ago, we were all aboard your Mother Ship having a conversation similar to this one conversation." 'Half of these peoples have come from all over the world just to be here." 'This could be settle among me and you, don't you agree Commander Qkunya."

"Madam President the seriousness of this matter of clowning the enemy to info trait there society for whatever reason, maybe importing explosives in their homeland." 'This alone could cause a serious aftermath upon your world for they belong to an alliance that may travel to this world and destroy you altogether Madam President."

"We are not bound by your rules or regulations Commander Qkunya, this is written in your handbook that we have studied." President Hillary said.

"Madam President, the world that you are trying to get to is 6 time the size of your planet and although the atmosphere is similar, you do not have the capability to travel such distance blindly thru space with no ways of refueling or the dietary that it takes to reprogram your body to survive beyond this world." 'Death will only become of you and even if you do manage to find your way to their planet somehow." 'The chance of you returning is almost none existence as I told you once Madam President, what happen with your world was a tragedy but we came to your aide and gave you a second chance at life." 'Do not leave this world in search of revenge, it will only bring you hardship and despair to your world." I.S.U.P Commander Qkunya said.

We sat listening to him speak of what could be our demise but we have been planning this too long to turned back and if I have been eating all this baby food just for nothing. Someone is going to die, there wasn't much anyone could say in our defense, and even the President sat in silence. I know wasn't the only one who feared what he was saying but he would know more than any alien we had accepted into our society. We know this was his job but we feared him contacting our invaders and informing them on our coming.

All we have been doing could be compromise before we even attempt to leave earth and if we made it, it would have all been for nothing. It would be like our own personal inner storm of destruction allowing them to get prepared. I could only hope that our Engineers and Scientists and Department of Defense work well together. We continue listening to him informed us that space is like our own flesh and blood body.

He told us how just when you think you have things figured out, something unknown appears just like our anatomy. Full of parasites virus and unknown diseases appearing from nothing.

"Commander Qkunya, if what you believe is true and if we do want destruction upon their world, who are you to tell us how to bring it." 'War is war Commander."

President Hillary explained.

"Madam President, if war is only war, than your existence would have ended with an unknown time."

Commander Qkunya responded with the same tone of voice.

"Commander Qkunya, you accused us of clowning our invaders to infect their world, if I recall." 'We had to come up with a Special Task force that had one job and that was destroying what was once human that had been transformed into basically zombies from contamination, some are still unknown to us alone with animals that was almost impossible to kill with small caliber arms."

"Madam President, we are aware of their tactics and these what you call zombies did go on to killing anything in their path but with time, this country alone with others did find ways of destroying them altogether." *'But with that being said, they were not clones and no violation of war found."*

This was going back and forth with no ending but as I remember, it affected everyone different, many doctors went on to become mad scientist and doing what they wanted behind closed doors. Most were destroyed by their own creations, it was easy to destroy the zombies because they walked the street in search of anything living. Warm blood is what they crave, mad doctors and scientists had become our biggest problem and animals of any kind made us their pray for their own survival as the President ask him if he remember those horrors that we faced?

"You come here and you tell us about what is fare and not, my country will suffer from now on as we have been infected with disease that appear without notice upon us." *'America has suffered, but no longer…my country want revenge upon our Alien Invaders that killed hundreds of thousands of China son's and daughter's that died for no reason." 'We do nothing to be destroyed for nothing Commander Qkunya and China will've its revenge, even if we go to their world ourselves." General Changsha spoke loudly.*

That moment we could here Japan and other European Nations agree along with Russia Ambassador yelling to the top of his voice. It was amazing how the I.S.U.P Commander Qkunya had remain calm without saying a negative word against strong opinions who was basically blaming him for what happen.

"Commander Qkunya, a lot has been said, maybe from mix emotions for whatever reason we all thank you for what you have done for our world." *'But I feel that your presence is no longer needed and* *we are big enough to handle our own problems as we have done before you arrived Commander."*

President Hillary said with a softer sexy tone in her voice.

"Madam President so much we need to discuss and so many answers I need from each of you, we have also monitor your spaceships beyond your atmosphere." 'You seem to be developing worm holes capability according to our diagnostic of your computer reading." 'This may give you what you need to reach their world but this is forbidden according to our regulation of space travel." 'Arneulians were even forbidding to use such means of travel due to our restrictions and the danger that comes with wormholes, even though it took them over 6 months to get to this world, they knew of the dangers."

Commander Qkunya explained.

"Commander Qkunya, why're you so against what we do on our so call tiny little planet and why do you just stay around monitoring us like kids?" Russian General Naukoff ask.

"Several months back General Naukoff, we monitor nuclear Japanese scientists entering your homeland and not long after we discovered electronic signals penetrating galaxy as far as the 4 Galilean Moons and only week's later Europa and Ganymede and Callisto star system and with this you must be aware of the deadly chlorine gases involving the Milasaura Planets."

Commander Qkunya stated.

"You spy on Russia and the Japanese scientist are on a joint force work program of human relations if you must know Commander Qkunya." Russian General Naukoff replied.

"I'm not any of your enemy but it is my job to help in anyway but not with direct involvement of your world." 'General Naukoff the Milasaura Planets are very dangerous to your atmosphere and even though the gases can be used as a source of fuel if control but it alone will kill anything that inhale it." 'We avoid it altogether because if it gets involve with our intake cooling system, our bodies have a less tolerance than yours." 'This for your own safety alone with this world." I.S.U.P Commander Qkunya said.

"You need to go back to your world Commander." Russian General Naukoff said loudly.

"We have been analyzing many of your electronic signals that you are incorporating into the technology we have giving you and it will do nothing but cause virus that you may not be able to control once you get away from earth gravitational field." 'If you leave earth blindly, you will travel into radioactive solar fields that you know nothing about and what this will do to your electronic is bring disruption that you want understand." 'It will be like your car breaking down without warning and never starting up again." I.S.U.P Commander Qkunya explained.

"Then you can give us the technology that we need to prevent such incident before happening. British Colonial Manchester said.

"I can't give you what is not approve by the Federation and when I request to, it will be denied because you are not ready for such technology yet." I.S.U.P Commander Qkunya said.

Silence had come about us, this commander wasn't going to get no information from anyone here no matter how many questions he ask or what he said. It didn't take him very long to figure this out, it didn't matter who he wanted here or from what country. We listen to him a bit longer before this had come to an end, it wasn't for nothing is all I could think because he had giving us some very valuable information. We watch him alone with his Staff depart from the White House while the President ask everyone else to remain behind for a moment.

"Commander Qkunya once again we know where we stand with them and we must be careful with whatever we do from this point on, is there any way that we can cut down on our radioactive signal from this point on?" President Hillary ask.

Several at one time answer that question and every answer was no, but it was understandable knowing how he wasn't on their technology level. That day ended but it was only a short time later before I was back in the White House knowing we were none down to about 20 days. We all sat around awaiting to hear what the President had to say.

"Ladies and Gentlemen, China has come forward with a plan they teamed up with some German scientists and between both countries, they have develop an electronic virus that could probably destroy the Mothership entire electrical computer data system." President Hillary said.

"How long will it be down?" Japan's General Niigata ask.

"There technology is so advance that it will give us time to get away from earth gravitational field or at least several hours maybe." President Hillary said.

"*So they may be powerless while watching us leave our own orbit, how long will it take to install this technology?*" Australian Colonial ask.

"**This will not be install in every vessel, there will be no need… this can be launch into their computer programs and from anywhere.**" '**There it will jam and scramble there electronic.**" **China Scientist Hangzhou responded.**

"*Rumor was that you had to be within 5 miles of their protective energy field.*" India Commander Jhansi ask.

"**Not true, if we sent it from home, we could use American satellite will penetrate the virus but this is where you come in President Hillary.**" '**You must open up their communication channel for the virus to infect their on board computer system.**" **China General Changsha said.**

"*I have something I want to add to this problem, we must do more than just shutting down there communication and you have no fore sure ideal that this will work.*" '*I say we attacked their Mothership and bring them from the sky for good all over the world at one time.*" Russian General Naukoff explained.

"**Ok, how're we supposed to do this Russian General Naukoff, please explain to me.**" **President Hillary ask.**

"*Russia has plan of bringing many satellites upon the Mothership and exploding them after you have infected there communication.*" '*It will disrupted them enough to penetrate them with our Star Wars Attack System, this will destroy them for good.* Russian General Naukoff said.

"**What about the aftermath of their retaliation and we agreed that, that system was dismantled years ago as we agreed to destroy ours?**" **President Hillary ask.**

"*Russia destroy nothing like you ignorant Americans and we will take their Commander, he knows much about space and we could use his wisdom.*" Russian General Naukoff said.

I'm sure everyone who sat here felt exactly what he was talking about.

"**There will be death from this journey and it should start with them Madam President.**" **I said.**

She said nothing but look my way like if I didn't even exist but she ask me to be here.

"**How're we to get the satellite that close to the Mother Ship?**" **President Hillary ask.**

Before anything could be answered I explained how we have several that need repair and they are already in their vicinity.

"I agree with this man." Russian General Naukoff said loudly.

The President just look on as the General Niigata saying how he is right because the nearest satellite is many miles away from the Mothership.

"If I may suggest an opinion of all of this?" Vice President Ayla asked.

That moment everyone gotten quiet as a mouse, this woman has been so against everything we every talked about.

"You may, what on your mind." President Hillary ask hostilely but polite at the same time.

"We have talked a lot about this massive invasion, but we have been through so much now from death to rebuilding and we have suffered so heavily and maybe we need to think about what we are about to do." Vice President Ayla said loudly.

The room became really quiet, no one said nothing as they sat back as Vice President Ayla gotten up walking around. This lady was the second most powerful in the world right now and she was heavily into politic before becoming what she is now.

"We have so many world leaders here today and what is decided from this point on will affect us for life and maybe what has been explained by the Commander Qkunya is right." 'I feel that if this adventure is pursued, we will destroyed what is left of our world without alien help from disease, famine, starvation unable to maintain the balance of life itself." 'Shouldn't this be time to rebuild worldwide?" Vice President Hillary ask.

Everyone kept quiet as no one responded back, there wasn't even a sound among any of us.

"Let make this happen because time is not on our side and I will give you anything you need to get this rolling and you all know that it has been moved up an entire week." President Hillary said.

There was nothing to be said from that moment on as the majority of us departed from the boardroom while listening to the Korean who seem to be having a problem with this plan from day one. Especially with our American leadership so they claim but we needed them along with their military to pull this off. I just wanted to get home now but as I was leaving,

I had been stop by Security and ask to return back to the boardroom. It wasn't a good sight once I entered, so much hostility within the blink of an eye but I could understand why but it was something about these North Koreans. If it was me I would have left them where they were but it wasn't. I stood back listening to the conversation and the President, she didn't seem to be happy with neither of them.

"Why would you do that and he gave you that authority?!" President Hillary ask.

"You…Americans are so weak but yet you want everything insight and you don't want to work to get it." 'We needed no authority, it was you who wanted us to be a part of this madness that you created…you came to us remember. Korean General Xinyang responded.

"But, what you done can killed each and every last one of them and did you think of the consequences if it was discovered by the Protectors?"

"So you do not approve of what we did I see but in reality you know we did the right thing and we have been monitoring each of them daily." Korean General Xinyang said.

"150 peoples from around the world and you took it upon yourself to put all of them in harm, did you do it to your own as well!" President Hillary ask.

"What we done is put the ball in your hand but we can initiate it from anywhere, including here to anyone of them or all at one time." Korean President Fengcheng

"You peoples are so interesting and evil at the same time." 'I want you to hear what they have done and want your opinion of what has happen." President Hillary said.

It was that moment after she told me that while I was waiting to see what General Xinyang was going to say. She had giving him a gesture like please tell him, maybe what I was about to hear was beyond me but I have been by her side form the beginning of this.

"We develop a newer way of tracking our prisoners once they were released but this device eventually involve into something greater." 'It was basically a Russian tracking device but we improve and made it undetectable and with time it became a listening device as well.

Everyone was medically giving this computer chip device that can be initiated by us." Korean General Xinyang explained.

"What're you talking about General Talley" I ask.

"What will it do to the 150 personnel aboard the alien vessel?" I asked."

"It can cause them to go complete crazy or explode causing them to die a horrible death." General Xinyang explained.

"Why would you do that?" I ask.

"Americans are the weakest link and if they were ever to be tortured or questioned or as we believe turned spy." 'It would be up to us to cure the problem as we never approve of this Interspace Foreign Exchange Work Program." 'I could do nothing but look at both of them before turning toward the President, it was wrong but overall a good ideal." General Xinyang explained.

"Madam President, you have over 600 peoples aboard their Mother Ship, it's basically a good ideal because they could cause a massive disruption within their entire space ship." 'If this happen, it could give us the upper hand easily and all you are losing is 600 lives compared to millions around the world." 'The few scientists aboard and doctors will be your biggest lost but if the Koreans can determine who dies, it's even better and they know the location of their assignments." I said.

She stood there looking at me but I could tell that her political advisors must to have already voice his opinion as he agreed with me. The look in her eyes only told me that this meeting was over, not to mention how she told the Marines to escort the President Fengcheng alone with his General Xinyang and their Staff to the north transporter room. I knew they wanted to get home just like I did but this was far from over.

Chapter 18

"36 HOURS"

So much coordination has been going on, it was now on 3 days before the most massive invasion within our world history. All the wars that has ever existed was only a drop in the bucket compared to what was about to happen in a short matter of time now. I myself has been at the White House every day from sun up to sundown as I found no reason to be there, but the President felt difference. So much had to be done on schedule and not a second later to keep suspicion down as they monitored everything we did it seem from every second of the day.

We brought together the smartest peoples from all over the world hoping for success while repairing arming our satellites with liquid explosive. It was something given to us from the Xilluinon, this was a species that has been nothing more than slaves since the destruction of their planet Xilnuon. Their intelligence alone made them highly dangerous but their silence made them unpredictable. Who knows what they had plan for us when this is all said and done knowing time itself was going to give us that answer.

No one was expendable from this mission, we even brought aboard some of the worst computer hackers known to man from state and federal prisons. Maybe this was one of the better decisions that the President had made when she had them transferred into the survival caves. That is where I met little Timothy, he was no older than 15 but someday schools will be name after this little hacker. His personality was nothing more than an irritation little bastard but his advance knowledge while working with other geeks.

They created this deadly computer virus designed for the Alien Mothership our stress levels was at its highest. Even more so among our teams that stood waiting for the signal to invade their alien ship defensive system. We all knew that if our plan fail our personnel will be in serious life threatening damage high above earth. So many countries stood waiting but it was General Bello who voice his opinion.

"We can be destroyed now or we can wait for one of these aliens left behind who will grow up lurking in the shadows and bring havoc on our world."

He was right and we really don't have much of a choice but to push forward with this invasion or deal with even a bigger invasion with time.

"We should fight now while everyone is pist off from the many deaths of family and friends we have lost from Arneulians Invaders years ago." I said.

I stood there at NASA Space Center with the Presidential Staff when they started moving our outer satellites into position outside the alien radar system.

"We have less than 20 minutes to do as much damage to their Mothership as possible and pray our jammers holds." Lt. CDR Leimer explain.

I could see over 1500 hundred pilots stood by around the world ready to destroy, they all new that death awaited them. Bravery at its best. So many prayers could be heard amongst us as I hope this doesn't fail knowing we didn't need another heavy loss.

"Sir we must secure this first worm hole." Ensign Hym shouted.

No one had no idea what he meant, maybe it was the high intensity stress level that was thicker than a big body blubber.

"3-2-1!" Lt. CDR Leimer counted.

All hell broke loose within the blink of an eye, the psychosis we heard would live in us until the day we die, so much pain from our own. We knew their bodies were burning from the inside out and there was nothing we could do but accept what was happening to them. 150 humans was going crazy while causing disruption as our alien invaders didn't know what the hell was going on among them.

"Give the order." President Hillary shouted.

Our satellite was on the move while our alien snitch had been silence, he never even knew what hit him knowing the aliens doing their best to maintain their station. Disruption and recklessness cause by us but our first satellite had been destroyed once it penetrated the alien airspace. Their defensive technology had no flaws as nothing came near them while noticing our President looking on. But if she didn't launch the awaiting carriers force this would be lost while we could hear the Admiral asking her what to do.

"Madam President." 'You must launch our Aircraft Carriers or all of this would have been for nothing.

She continue to hesitate until he yelled even louder.

"Admiral, launch your Aircraft Carriers." President Hillary shouted.

There was no turning back, we could see them moving from 25 miles away toward the Mothership at full speed. It wasn't long after China Russia Mexico Canada Japan and British all join in the fight. Universal Protectors put up a good fight but it was too many for them to handle. Every country has their job of disarmament their massive Mothership but after a fierce battle, it was over.

We had to praise the Japanese for knocking out there communication and China for intercepting there emergency stress alerts. When it was all said and done, we enter their ship and to see so many that didn't die was a sight to see as we had to take their life as we saw fit. We left the Australians and a large African force that would take control of their Mothership. Several days had passed before we were all back in the White discussing what just happen. I accommodated the President to one of our hidden prison facilities.

"Madam President...what you have done is a major violation and you will be responsible, in fact this entire world will."

"Commander Qkunya we are preserving our species and im sure you can understand that."

"You think you would get away with what you have done?"

"Commander Qkunya we don't have time to argue and we need your help with jumping space and time."

"Madam President we gave you technology but not that kind, it never happen in your lifetime."

"Commander Qkunya we do." President Hillary said loudly.

He doubted her unto she shown him proof, he was nothing but surprise.

"Madam President how can this be?"

I saw nothing but fascination in his eyes, if he would not had proof, they was no way this was believable.

"Commander Qkunya we need your help jumping thru time and space using your worm holes."

"Madam President I will not help you or my Staff."

"Commander Qkunya you will or you and your Staff will die, is that what you want Commander Qkunya?!"

"Madam President you send your troops to die but you stay behind, your existence is cowardly and I have no honor for cowards."

"Commander Qkunya you will you help us and if not you, than your crew and you will die!' Right here and right now!"

"Madam President I will not, nor will my team."

It was that moment, he had this crazy look in his eyes as he gotten up walking around but something about him was nonviolence this time. We keyed in on his awkward movement and within a blink of an eye shot four of his own members before pulling the trigger on himself. But his weapon misfired, it was that moment our Secret Service Agents and Security had taking him down.

"Idiot!"

President Hillary shouted but she could do nothing but look down on as they were cuffing him up before bringing him to his feet. The look she had giving him was like if she wanted to take his life herself.

"Take him away and lock him up!" President Hillary shouted.

Silence had come about us as we stood around looking at each other.

"Any ideas now." President Hillary ask.

Many voice their opinion but that was the least of our problems.

"You need to take him by force and he will be force by honor to help you." Blaskin said.

Much later she made her way toward Commander Qkunya as she now stood before him.

"Commander Qkunya we decided to take you with us and if you want to see your world." 'I advise you to cooperate and we have all your technology for the past years and we are now interrogating the remainder of you Staff."

"Not one will give you information Madam President."

"Maybe so Commander Qkunya."

Chapter 19

"Departure"

Over 1000 Military Ships Cargo-Planes, Ocean Liners and Cruise-Ships anything that was big enough to transport. This was nothing more than amazing sight I ever seen in my life as many more from around the world became one. This was history in the making as were to become the largest worldwide invasion all under one command of a fiery redheaded woman. Commander Qkunya couldn't believe his eyes, the sight of what hovered above him as we stood.

I knew he wondered how in the hell did he miss this transformation taking place right underneath his nose, even more so on a scale this large. But not once did he make a sound, not a single word came from his mouth as he stood looking on. He looked as if he was living statue displaying honor for all who look upon him.

"Admiral…let go." President Hillary said.

That moment the sound of nuclear propulsion of over 100.000 vessels sounded like the gates of hell defying gravity lifting from the oceans into the atmosphere as we were leaving the world behind into the darken space. It didn't take long as we pulled away from earth gravitational field as the earth was now getting smaller. Communication was the key as the third day was approaching as we pushed deeper into our solar system. It wasn't long after, we were moving into our first warm hole and that was going to be the beginning of this mission.

So much fascination, so much skill of navigation as we were now only one day away from a point that we needed to be. So much was beyond our sight and now it was right before our face, it was amazing the distance were from earth. The first day was the worst but the Vertillian stepped up just as they said they would. Their navigational knowledge lead this entire fleet through our solar system.

It seem to be the most difficult from the meteor showers to unknown gases that destroyed several of our lead ships. Death had come at them without warning or escape, we lost more than 10 ships from that alone and at least another 30 from mechanical failure. This was only the beginning as we continue this long journey that was ahead of us. We had come upon the Kike Stars that painted a never ending breath taking pictures.

Our President intervene from time to time because our educated space-age college kids thought they were smarter than the aliens who had become our navigational expert. It was understandable since we come from two different mathematical systems, not to mention that this was all new to us. I had nothing to say from the moment we left, this was so far from my lane as I was nothing more than an idiot to any question asked about traveling through space. It wasn't long after the Captain of the ship had inform us that another 6 ships from Mexico had fallen back due to mechanical engine failure.

My personal opinion is that the U.S.S. Beto alone with U.S.S. Quan Gonzalez Chavez should have stayed earthbound floating off their white sandy drug infested coastline protecting the mafia drug route. If this was to keep happen, we want have nothing going thru the worm-hole, it alone had been computed that we were going to lose a large portion of our force. Once that little unauthorized information had started to travel. It brought nothing but panic and fear to the crew because they feared the death that was going to come alone with it.

I myself tried not to think of it although it bother me as well but being Special Force's, it taught me that death could come to you at any point in your life. The second day we had taking on this form of sickness but it was an easy cure as we had been instructed to take aspirins daily. I moved about this carrier amongst the sailors and soldiers having nothing but respect for each of them. Our…Commander seem to be fearless.

"Good morning Commander Qkunya."

He just stood there looking at President Hillary while saying nothing.

"In a few hours Commander Qkunya, we will be approaching our first warm-hole and we can you really use your help navigating our way through it." 'Not to mention that don't know much about it and you do, it really would be nice if you come aboard especially right now Commander Qkunya."

He stood in silence while looking like if he wasn't even here but I could tell that the President didn't have time for his games or was she going to waste her time with him.

"Okay Commander Qkunya, I see where you stand but I had to have you with us and for that I apologize from my heart." 'But you give me no choice now in what I have to do." 'As long as you are here Commander Qkunya, I would do my best to give you fair treatment and keep you healthy and I hope that you change your mind but I have a ship to navigate." 'I must leave but we have others but it would be nice to have you with us."

It was that moment she had taking a few steps and stop.

"Commander Qkunya, I should be receiving information on your crew, I will give you the update as soon as I get the information." President Hillary said.

She ask me to followed her, we left him standing there knowing this was nothing more than politics, this was her strategy to get him to come aboard.

"Madam President, we don't know much about his weakness but I think you should limit his food ration until he come aboard." I suggested.

"We took him from everything he has ever known and we brought him with us by force, his silence will remain until he realized that this is real." President Hillary said.

There wasn't much for me to say from that point because in many ways she was correct and it was best that I watch my words with this woman.

"We have a meeting in Ready Room with several world leaders, I want you to be there, so don't get lost." President Hillary said.

I gotten to my birthing quarter feeling tired and rest was what I needed but somehow I knew what happening. My over sleeping wasn't good as I had arrived late with all eyes on me from these world leaders being transported back to their ships.

"You need to get ready for the worm-hole."

"Yes Madam President."

"It was all I could say while getting in my ass but it was expected and she was the boss.

"Have you been eating?"

"Madam President that food is horrible."

"You have to get use to digesting it."

We all had been giving food design for astronauts and now it was been redesign for our massive invading force.

"You are aware that we spent multibillion-dollars on this worldwide program and even im not enjoying it but it something we must all do before leaving."

"I will try but it like eating flavored toothpaste." I said.

"Get over it, you are a soldier, shit everything involving this mission has to be either altered or redesigned even the clothes were wearing now!" President said."

Chapter 20

"ARRIVED"

This journey had taken longer than we expect, 6 months has now past us and our food supply was dwindling down to nothing. We have seen some amazing as well as suffering from computer malfunctions to normal wear and tear within ourselves. Nearly 30% of our fighting force and 14% of our vessels has been lost, some say with the amount of travel we have done, it wasn't bad. I say different knowing we are going into another zone that we know little about but we had two species known as the Ziku and Ruzeuna who were known for slave trading before their world was invaded and destroyed by the Arneulians...our invaders.

Both species were now forced into survival but from what we have gathered, they wanted some form of payback of any kind. Before our third worm hole jumped, we had come upon their distress signal as we welcome them aboard. They showed so much fear as we enter but within 3days time with their help, we threw what was known as the Dead Star System, it was the pathway into the Tunnel of Death. We were told of its storms of exploding unknown gasses that cluster together like floating clouds of our world.

We had no choice but to pushed forward or face an electrical storm that would have destroyed us all for sure, it was nothing more than scary from beginning to end. Every ship had to minimize all electrical as we moved through space like lighting through the sky only to be spit out hours later. When it was all said and done, we lost more ships due mechanical failure knowing we should have slowed down. So much has happen as we made our way to the most unhibited darkest part of their world that was 6 times larger than earth.

Numerous suns and moons, our world seem perfect compared to this unknown planet. We invaded them with over 75.000 ships and had another 225.000 vessels from aircrafts tanks and war vehicles from around the worlds. Soldiers of every walks of life was ready for payback and now seem motivated to fight to the death. It wasn't even a day of settling in before we held our first world meeting of the leaders, so much planning had been done as everyone was welcome aboard the U.S.S Nimitz.

She took a beating from her mighty structure to her paint nearly stripped from her body like if she had been sand blasted repeatedly.

I watched many come thru the transporter to discuss plans and strategy but all I heard was bickering while debating before President had enough and brought it to an end. But we all knew that this wasn't the time and it was only a matter of time before we are discovered no matter how much we scramble there detection signals.

"We ole thanks to Ruzeuna who guided us in undetected thru the Nyrou Solar System, it was better that we pushed thru than trying to go around it and suffer even an heavier loss from what was explained to us."

"Your soldiers will be remembered, even among our world when we get back home." President Hillary said.

"General, we didn't have time to mourn your 3000 loss but out of respect I ask our Catholic Priest to say a prayer in their honor." President Hillary said.

I listen as the Romania General Buccuresti agreed, it was that moment our Priest Gonzalez lead us in prayer, I wasn't a catholic neither was many others but we dropped our heads in silence out of respect I guess.

"Now we have an invasion to plan knowing this world is six time larger than our but the majority of it is land." 'Keiahwau who sit among us made detail strategic maps that are being distributed defines it main headquarters along with key cities and industries locations about this world." 'They will explain more of this world." President Hillary said.

We listen to this reptilian, they were very fascinated and agile in the water but what was impressive was the depth they could dive. There tongue was thick that it words could hardly be understood. The *Lkuion* were a big help, their appearance was as if they were direct predators with their sculpture human like muscular bodies. It was hard to understand how they were enslaved by our invaders, we listen of their weakness but their strength came in numbers. They mentality was that of wolves and a for sure way to end the fight was to killing their leaders to end the fight.

"I have a 172000 troops and all I need to know is how to deploy them and I want no suicide mission because I intend to bring my sons back home to their families." 'Do we have an understanding?" Russian General Naukoff said aggressively without hesitation.

"General Naukoff, 'We are all sacrificing, just being here and there are no suicide mission here." President Hillary shouted back even louder.

"Americans play too many games and my sons will not be a part of your games, they will be homes with their families when this invasion is done." Russian General Naukoff said even louder.

"General Naukoff, we are all in this together and if you don't come here to do what we came here to do, you don't have to worry about getting your sons home," 'because we probably want have one to go back to." President Hillary said even louder.

"Humans, there are no enemies here among us, we have come very far through obstacles that where meant to destroy us." 'Now we must become one with each other." Fuomi Leader Oromia said mildly.

Everyone had gotten quiet after that until the Russian General Naukoff look at the President and told her that not one of his troops will move without him been a part of their decision making. She said nothing back in response to his outburst.

"We must attack their water supply while it is not heavily guarded, it must be poison and this must be done at the same time but you must understand that humans will be affected as well, unless you have enough to sustain you until your return home. Fuomi Leader Oromia said softly.

"We need to secure our supply first." China Emperor shouted loudly.

"Our ships can hold large amount of water in our tanks." Japanese General Kitayushu responded.

"We are to trust you with our lives, we will store our own!" Russian General Naukoff, shouted.

That moment, the sound of many country leaders had begun to argue among each other about their past and future events. It was like neither one trusted each other until silence had come about the room as everyone held their ears from the Fuomi high pitch sound waves. It was their defensive technique.

"We must become one with each other or we are destine to die here as enemies among each other." Fuomi Leader Oromia responded none aggressive.

"We will all store our own supply." President Hillary shouted loudly.

Everyone agreed.

"This attack must happen soon before we are discover." Fuomi Leader Oromia said in a low tone of voice.

"This world has more water than our world but is it drinkable?" President Hillary ask.

"No, this salt water will not kill you but the parasites that live within will eat you from the inside out, it must be boil before consumption." 'We must travel more inland for fresh water." Fuomi Leader Oromia responded.

We watch the Fuomi plot a course, very risky and several hours away, hoping we are not expose.

"You must fly ground level at all times no matter what and destroy any alien craft you come in contact with without hesitation." 'You cannot risk exposure and also this part of the planet should give you no resistance and from my understanding. 'Nothing lives in this area." Fuomi Leader Oromia explained.

"How do you know of this?" China Emperor Nanchang ask.

"My culture work the underground mines here for years as slaves, they conquered our world and with time we formed a special sight of seeing in darkness." 'This is why my eyes glow in darkness and im familiar with this region and I was a slave that gave all I had to be aboard that spaceship that accidently landed in your world." Fuomi Leader Oromia explained none hostile.

"How long does it take to pump this water?" Russian General Naukoff ask loudly.

"It settled, we move out in a few hours with anything designed to carry water with escorting battleships, this is something we didn't prepare for but it better to be safe than not." President Hillary said.

The Russian General Naukoff stood there looking at everyone, I guess he wanted his answer as he ask again and she said nothing for the moment but just looked his way.

"General Naukoff, we don't have time to debate, pump whatever you can, infect can you get working on it now and we could use your battleships as escorts for safety." President Hillary ask.

"You are a woman built to have babies and prepare food for man and you know nothing about an invasion or controlling a force this large." 'You want to move into the unknown, this takes strategy and strategic planning." Russian General Naukoff shouted.

"General Naukoff, we are leaving with or without you, so I suggest you get your shit together ASAP and my Generals will see that my orders are carried out!" 'Get your shit together General Naukoff, in fact, that an order." President Hillary responded back.

This was going to be more than interesting as this meeting had come to an end, im thinking that more than 150 ships may be taking on water, if all goes well before returning. I had been ask to travel alone, not that I wanted to as we had departed upon this 3 hour mission. Our first 2 hours was nothing more than direct movement as we hover above a few hundred feet off the ground for nothing more than safety. The moment we came across water, we dropped down to about 50feet once we gotten to water before entering land again.

We moved about 100 miles per hour but with so much open land it seem even slower, this gravitational field was much different than ours. Fuomi knew exactly what they were doing, we made it undetected as we hovered aboard this massive inland fresh water lake. Once we started pumping, it didn't take long as we done what we had to before leaving this area. The only hard thing about pumping was this spongy type fish that kept clogging up the pumps.

We were told of the death they could bring from touch and if eaten, the stuff we had come in contact with was unbelievable. In the process we lost several tanker from mechanical failure but she had already known it. Knowing now she wanted to hear it from the horse's mouth but we left no one behind, we even had to it sink them before leaving.

Chapter 21

"Dakarion"

That day the President spoke to 2 *Dakarion* on them joining us, the Fuomi who was our translators wasn't understanding how we ask for their help. Both were all about riches and nothing more as they agreed only if they could be free when it was all said and done. But the Fuomi insisted they be restrained the entire time and monitored them none stop but we had bigger issues, they were like vultures wanting to feed on us basically. The President didn't know how to respond to their sicken request, there massive sized and high metabolism could devour a human every third day easily. Our General Talley didn't know how to react to it either, but we needed their help.

"I have traitors among my crew that had been name during the Alien Invasion." Russian General Naukoff said.

He told us that we can do with them as they please dead or alive.

"They prefer them alive and warm." Fuomi Leader Oromia explain grossly.

There was no way we were ever going to understand their language but we were explained how they need to feed now. It been nothing no more than a mission just to keep them fed and now she was giving into their gross craving for human flesh. I could hear the Russian General talking to his Major about bringing his two traitors and 3 worthless civilians of his to our carrier. This was something I had no desire to see if it was to take place, I could only hope they kill them before giving them over.

Chapter 22

"BUEROXEN"

We had taken lead along the side of the U.S.S Texas while been trailed by a small force, that moment something had come over the radar. It was getting closer by the second but nothing could be seen in the distance or near. Our light flashed none stop as we knew something was before us, the Captain bought our entire fleet to a stop as we now drifted. Within the blink of an eye something appeared from thin air and then two more to the left and the right of it.

There ship look warrior like as they appeared on our monitor system, once again we encountered another unknown language we never heard before. We had all this technology and yet we were still new to it as we look toward the Fuomi for help. One of the crew members had gotten the President some coffee, her eyes gotten big as she shook nervously. "Bueroxen!" She responded.

"Kuoanyi who are they?"

"*President Hillary…killers.*"

We couldn't understand them, even the Fuomi only knew bits of their language as Kuoanyi had done something we never expected.

"Do you know what you are doing Kuoanyi?"

"*Yes President.*" *Kuoanyi responded.*

We said nothing but watch her messing with the computer system.

"Bueroxen are very impatient President Hilleary" ***"Take your time Kuoanyi."***

"*Almost done President Hilleary!*"

What we thought was only a slave had decoded this computer to ware we could communicate with the Bueroxen.

"Who are you and why you are in this unauthorized zone, this is our solar system." Bueroxen ask.

"We are travelers passing thru and this area is unknown to us and we bring you no harm." 'It would be nice to have your permission to past thru this region." President Hillary ask.

"Why ask what you have already done by force?" Bueroxen Commander said aggressively.

President sat for a brief second.

"Be prepared to be boarded or destroyed." Bueroxen Commander said even more aggressive.

"You don't have my permission." President Hillary said.

"You have only a brief moment to decide of be fired upon and you will all die!"

It was that moment she look toward the Fuomi for answers while ordering the Russian to stand who had Japan and China waiting for orders to attack.

"They will destroy you and if you fire back, they will alert their armies who can't be far behind as they travel in aggressive packs." Fuomi Leader Oromia explained.

"We move in and fire!" Russian General Naukoff, shouted.

"Stand down General Naukoff and hold your position!" President Hillary shouted loudly.

"General have your soldiers to bring the Universal Protector here ASAP, right now." President Hilary ordered. "Priest, I need your collar now." President ask somewhat politely.

He look so puzzled while she ask him again, it was that moment we watched him removed it before handing it over. It was only a moment later that they brought in the Universal Commander as we watched the President move his way.

"Listen here, this is a device that is designed to decapitate you within in seconds if giving the command, this is how it work...acid will dissolve into your flesh causing a brutal death that I hope doesn't happen any time soon." 'Now we have Bueroxen about to enter our ship any minute and im sure you know what they are capable of and

if you really like to keep the peace." "This'll prove it plus it will keep you alive to deal with us later." President Hillary said.

"General, they are hailing us again." Lt said.

"Open the channel display screen." General Talley said.

"Give us your transfer code, so we may come aboard or prepared to be fired upon." Bueroxen Commander said loudly.

It was that moment we listen to the Lt. inform us that they are positioning their weapons targeting certain areas at our ship.

"Give them the codes and bring them to transporter One." President Hillary order her Lt.

It was that moment that we could do nothing but wait for their arrival, they were nothing more than impressive from their shiny detail uniforms. It alone told us that they feared nothing, they massive 6ft structure with pitch black midnight eyes and there red skin tone was like if they were the devil themselves. They had to be warriors from birth, even more so how their weapons seem to be built directly for each of them, perfection at its best.

"My name is Commodore Esia Nuyigypt of the Star Ship Ebjatau and why you are here in our solar system?"

Silence had come about us as he looked about.

"I'm the President of the United States Of America. President Hillary said.

"Answer my question!"

"Commodore Esia Nuyigypt, it is an honor to meet you and like I said, this is an unknown area to us and we are only passing thru." President replied.

These was nothing but warriors by nature, it was like if he didn't even care to hear nothing while his soldiers stood awaiting his every command to be carried out. Each one could easily taking several of us at a time.

"Commodore Esia Nuyigypt, this is my General Talley alone with Universal Protector Qkunya" President Hillary said.

That moment all 6 of them bow their heads including the Commodore Esia Nuyigypt for a brief moment.

"My apology Qkunya …if I know you were aboard, this would not have happen knowing you were on board this strange unknown

Starship and may we do anything for you." Commodore Esia Nuyigypt ask.

"Yes…Commodore Esia Nuyigypt, we need approval to pass thru your solar system." President Hillary replied.

That moment silence had surface among us.

"Is that what you require Qkunya" Commodore Esia Nuyigypt ask.

"Yes, an escorting signal upon our fleet would be satisfactory Commodore Esia Nuyigypt." Universal Protector ask.

"You will have what you ask for Qkunya but beware of the worm-holes, they have been very unpredictable." Commodore Esia Nuyigypt said.

Nothing more had been said as they return to the transporter to be beam back to their Starship Ebjatau, the sight of them leaving was nothing more than a relief. But we had no ideal about what our Protector Qkunya and Commodore Esia Nuyigypt was talking about before his departure. We could only hope there discussion don't come back to bite us in our ass. We entered their planetary system and now we could see why they protected this world like if their life depended on it.

It was nothing more than amazing, some of these planetary islands were different sizes and some was no bigger thn Texas while others was equal to our earth and some even bigger. They had no sun but somehow this colorful star systems was brighter than our own sun. Their population was in the billions just like the stars that surrounded this unknown strangeness as we travel for at least three months just to get through the universe alone with many surprising solar storms.

It was one of the main reasons why we had to slow down so much and sometimes even wait for days at a time. They came without notice and erupted like volcanoes destroying us like hurricanes and tornadoes on earth. We were told death was for sure to follow, more than we can handle. Just before we entered the Darken Galaxy, the Bueroxen *Commander* had befriended us for the strength they saw within our Species.

We are allowed to enter their last remaining planet that sat on their outer solar system called the Nxueh. We were allowed to stay as long as it took to get our Fleet ready for travel back home, there world was nothing more than impressive yet civilized. We headed toward the Auguanau Star System, it was the place that we finally departed the Bueroxen Planetary

Solar System. It was also the beginning of another destiny of what I was told was a never ending journey.

But according to the Dakarion, it was one of the worst places to be in this star system, it was like if the plague made its home here. Yet we were heading directly into the belly of the beast. We travel more than three days and somehow we blew pass the warm-hole. Maybe our navigational system was off due to solar flares storm that we couldn't avoid. Our President wanted to know how could this happened but the Dakarion explained how wormholes are very unstable.

"Disruption of the magnetics field can cause major interference, you thought you could take our technology and make it work for you." **Universal Commander Qkunya said.**

"You can lead us out of here Commander Qkunya instead of talking." *President Hillary said loudly.*

Everyone could tell that she was now highly frustrated with several nations all depending on her.

"You fail to realized that we constantly are testing worm-hole and with thousands of year behind us, we have profected what you assumed will never change but worm-holes are life living creatures with minds of their own." **Universal Commander Qkunya said.**

"What the worst can happen now?" President Hillary ask.

"Your ignorance has entered a Galaxy Star System that has nothing to do with the Bueroxen or our Federation, this area operates without remorse and the out-come is unknown attacks but due to your massive size." *'You may face devastation attempts without notice, the technology of some of these Alien Pirates Species are notorious killers that we don't even know much about and there advance operation make them dangerous to your blinded fleet."* **Universal Protector Qkunya said.**

Silence had come about the bridge as the President ask that all available channels be open at once.

"Im aware of the Zaxutu Bihego and the Fyminum, if you are contact by any of these…destroy them immediately because there are killers." Kuoanyi said.

"Kuoanyi you are appearing to be great importance to us without notice." President Hilleary said.

"All hands…tis is Fleet Commander President of the United States… we have enter an unknown galaxy star system that are known to be the worst of the worst." 'There technology maybe far advance than ours and they maybe undetected by our radar, so I ask you to be on a higher alert until told difference." 'Fleet Commander out."

"Commander Qkunya should we turned around?" President Hillary ask.

"Madam President you can do as you chose but you have two choices and that is achievement or failure." Universal Commander Qkunya said.

"So…Commander Qkunya you don't know?" President Hillary ask.

"Fleet Commander I advise you to keep forward, turning back may put many lives in danger, there is a great solar storm approaching from the rear." Fuomi Leader Oromia said.

"How do you know this?" Russian General Naukoff ask.

"It is detected upon our skin, as we swim beneath currents that your submarine dream about." 'Our skin is very sensitive to the universe and your scanner may not pick this storm on your radar." Fuomi Leader Oromia responded.

"None sense, you are nothing special neither are you Americans, now I see why it took you so many years to fight your Vietnam war and for what?" 'You still lost. Russian General Naukoff said loudly.

"This not the time Genera Naukoff!" President Hillary said.

"This the time and I have over 35% of my sons alive because of your ignorance and failure to be a Leaders of Nations!" 'Mother Russia is the stronger country and from this point on, I'm taking Fleet Command of this mission of getting us home." Russian General Naukoff said.

"Stand down General." President Hillary shouted.

"You don't even have communication with the Bueroxen anymore and your incompetence has gotten us lost." 'I gave you directions to the worn-hole but you listen to these traitors among us." General Naukoff shouted even louder.

"General Naukoff, you will stand down now!" President Hillary shouted.

That moment everyone gotten silence as the President gotten only inches from his face looking up at the 6ft 3 massive man. The sound of his soldiers had chamber their weapons, it cause our soldiers to do the same.

It was nothing but the scariest sound ever that had taken over the silence, but she had done nothing but stand there looking up at him. This one seem to have to be on some kind of suicidal mission, it was that moment the General Naukoff stood there looking down at her.

This man wasn't just an office General, when his men went out on suicidal missions, he fought alone with them. I personally thought that the President has set him up for failure hoping that he died on the battlefield. But he survived every time.

"Stand down General Naukoff or I will put you down myself." President Hillary shouted.

"You are lost and I will get us home from now." General Naukoff shouted down at her.

"We aren't lost!" President Hillary said loudly.

"This mission is now under my command." General Naukoff shouted even louder

It was that moment she moved in even closer looking up at him with no fear whatsoever.

"You will do as I say General Naukoff from this point on or I will have you on charges for disobeying a direct order from your Commanding Fleet Officer." President Hillary said.

"Your incompetence is not accepted by Mother Russia from this second on." General Naukoff shouted down at her.

This was getting completely out of control and no one was stepping between these two power houses that had the ability to destroy each other in the blink of an eye.

"Authority has been giving to me by a unanimous vote including your own Russian President who instructed your loyalty to me." 'Do you have a problem with my authority General Naukoff?" President Hilary ask.

That moment time felt like it just frozen, nothing but silence surrounded us as this massive man said nothing but look down at her. If looks could kill our President would not be standing right now.

"Your incompetence gives me the authority to override Presidential authority for the better of Mother Russia." 'As of now, I no longer follow your incompetence authority, your leadership is beneath me and Russia resigned from this campaign as of now." 'You are going

to transfer me back to my Aircraft Carrier." General Naukoff said loudly.

Nothing about what just happened was good, what he just done could cause a domino effect easily and we needed to be as one. It's not good to be an individual right now especially so far from home plus we just been weakened as a force.

"Good day General Naukoff and I wish you luck on getting home." President Hillary said.

There was nothing we could do but watch him leave reducing our fighting force becoming two individual armies.

Chapter 23

❧

"Auga Naux Solar System"

❧

Several days passed and we have lost complete communication with General Naukoff but even I knew the moment he turned around in search of the warm hole. He wasn't coming back as we were headed into the Auga Naux Solar System, it was the first time that we have actually slow down to study what was before us. It was decided that we had no choice but to push through as one and with that being said. We have lost contact with several nations including Japan China and surprisingly Greece and Mongolia, it only taken a moment before they decide to do the same thing as Russian General Naukoff.

Our President were losing control and there wasn't much she could do about it but accept what was happening to our Fleet. I myself never expected any of this to happen, we were so far with home and we can through the hardest part and actually made past the Invasion. They were nothing more than a loss knowing 60% of soldiers died during the war but that's what come with fighting an aggressive war. But we kept up our high spirits, even though we were dying daily.

Japan and China sacrifice everything to make this happen from my point of view and I could only hope that history is written the way it happen. We continued moving forward the best we could while fighting in packs that kept us stronger than as an individual. We tried to avoid having heroes but with so much suffering, there was many who stood out even among uncontrollable diseases that took us in great numbers without warning. So many invasions we force upon our enemies also brought viruses upon us as well.

Maybe that why so many fought without fear, it was better to die fighting than from outlandish foreign disease, that done things to our body that you would not want to imagine. So many have seen their friends die so far from home from the simplest cold not much less than what this mission had thrown at us. So much we have prepared for the sickness and the death that we endure from the moment we left wasn't. That night Capt. Lance didn't get a wink of sleep as he stayed on the bridge pushing deeper into the solar system and when he finally did close his eyes.

His radar lite up flashing none stop, our leadership have been fired upon. We instantly went into code red, it was our highest alert as everyone gotten up manning their battle stations. We were now being fired upon as we were order to fired back, it was nothing for them to get past our defense with the speed of the crafts. But our large numbers was under estimated as we appear like ghosts blasting down from the sky until they retreated into the distance darkness.

We when it was all said and done, we suffered once more losing over 13 ships along with the majority of its personnel. We only managed to get so many transported before death consumed them, our ship was already overpopulated as we pushed on. We suffered heavily, even more so with all this new technology that has been poorly maintain since we been giving it. What we had was just before our time along with the proper maintenance as this moment alone left us with the abandonment of another 14 ships.

It was nothing more than another great loss as we strip them down and took only what we needed. The sight of what we were was becoming nothing more than space garbage with time as we continue week after week into this solar system. It alone have become an overall destroyer from that battle that we enter to disease that found their way into our ventilation system. Civilians that we had a board have become Soldiers and Soldiers have become Officers and Officers have become Ship Commanders.

Death that we were facing wasn't discriminatory as we found sickness from every direction. Our ground forces fought many battles up close and personal mostly, so much bravery while knowing we were the aggressors fighting against defending fighting force. Both were relentless but we also picked up many unknown viruses from hand-to-hand combat. Our medicine had no cure according to our overnight doctors and now anyone who knew anything about medicine.

So many unknown viruses was killing us without warning but even I knew that this was nothing more than normal as we invaded there world. But now they are coming to life and destroying us little by little, it gotten so bad that we actually force personnel to distant planets. It was nothing but the worst feeling ever to leave Americans behind living within isolation and only the food of the carry. Our medical wards should have been a place for healing but mostly it was death that they faced, some even feared going the minute they were told.

We were still so far from home and yet so many small battles along with defending ourselves and destroying obstacles, they could bring us harm. We seem to be running low on high power ammunition, every nation was almost for themselves now and survival was becoming our only friend instead of each other. It wasn't long after, a major meeting had been call and we were summon and to my belief I had a feeling that we were going to be the main host of the party for some strange reason.

I remember that day vividly as we had been escorted to our seats, I could only hope that the President calm down some at least and be more civilized to everyone. Her attitude was as if she had a constant volcano flow destroying everything around as I even wonder how long could this rag thing last. So much had been said.

"Commander Qkunya what should we do?"

"Madam President we know nothing of this forbidden of limit galaxy known as the Auga Naux is similar to an unexplored maze that goes forever." *'You humans destroy an entire species leaving almost nothing...your nuclear bombs, I warn you that you did not care and you pursue this evil and now you find yourself in hell waiting to be picked off until you are no more."*

"Commander Qkunya we need your help to get out of the solar system, under your laws you have to give us advice and no one knows this area better than you." 'Not even the Dakarion."

"Madam President you have to send a distress signal nonstop from every ship that has the capability, it will be picked up." 'but at the same time every spaceship is at risk of being destroyed or be taken."

"There has to be a better way, Commander Qkunya!"

"*Madam President so many of your peoples have died and if you want to get home, you need to do as I say because you are too far from home. No one will ever know your whereabouts.*

"**Commander Qkunya there are several planets near.**" *Dakarion said are you familiar with these planets?*"

"**Madam President the Auga Naux will destroy you upon contact, they are fierce predators destroying everything in sight and known for leaving nothing alive.**"

That moment everyone gotten quiet while looking at the President who had the world on her shoulders.

"**Commander Qkunya can we sell to their world?**"

"*No Madam President, they take no prisoners and they help no one, the only allegiance is to themselves…You don't want to sell to their world.*" *Universal Commander Qkunya said.*

We watched him move towards the map system pointing out an area that they are known to be, it was a first time he spoke of plotting a course to an unknown region.

"**Madam President we must carefully avoid heavy conflict at all cost and if we do, we must not try to fight or we will find our way into a world of death.**"

"*Commander Qkunya we must not fight, even if fired upon.*" *President Hillary said.*

"**President Hillary it is no secret that we are here, the battles that you have fought is what kept you alive this long.**" *Fuomi Leader Oromia said.*

"*This meeting has ended but I need only world leaders to stay behind, the rest of you get some sleep including you as well Mr. Bailey.*" *President Hillary said.*

There was nothing no one could say as we were being escorted out leaving them alone behind closed doors as we saw several more weeks pass. Only death had come to us, even our President has been injured from some Qwzouri soldier who meet his death from Marines. General Talley was now in command but the British had complete control of the mission. We were almost completely out of the loop as it didn't take us long to realize that the Qwzouri was fierce and destructive.

They kept attacking us without warning, most of our radar has been destroyed but we continue to fight to the best of our ability. Our aircrafts were almost down to nothing knowing most were destroyed from the Arneulians Defensive System. We done what we could to protect our Carriers even with been moved to the outer perimeter by the British. Battleships and Destroyers was our last hope but with so many small battles and many small attacks.

We were being wipe out on purpose it seems in this ocean of space with limited faulty communication knowing our enemies knew of this somehow. We fought and fought many losing battles, it was like if we were destroying ourselves while our President received daily report. General Talley had taking some unknown psychological illness, his judgement was now to be questions. His ability to function has caused the British to take full command, our fighting style change into this guerrilla tactics.

We were now the aggressors, it was our jobs to destroy the Auga Naux defensively before coming upon their planet. Our President had been advised by her Staff that several alien species told us not to fight or even fire upon the Auga Naux but concentrate all fire power toward the Qwzouri if we wanted to survive. President Hillary had taken their advice as we turned our ships as we around focusing on the Qwzouri. We believe that even they must to have been shock, we hope this sent a strong message out to the Auga Naux.

Death awaited us to see the outcome for both alien species were fierce but the Auga Naux came like the leaves on a tree. It didn't take long before the Qwzouri retreated into the darkness leaving us to deal with the aftermath of this madness.

Chapter 24

"Contact"

They had kept their distance for several days as we drifted knowing that we were in some kind of restricted space. There was no escaping because our engines and electronic had been disabled down to just enough to survive somehow. It was the third day that they made contact with us before eventually coming aboard the USS Nimitz in force. We knew that trying to fight with them was an impossible waste of time, maybe they studied our entire defensive system.

They knew that we were no more of a threat to them than a grain of sand to an ocean. I wasn't a part of our leaders meeting but I witnessed the aftermath as we never entered the planet while given us aide. This massive ship they dispatched to us was nothing more than amazing from the size to the technology. Once inside, it would take the average human months to explore by foot easily. We even received medical attention from our death threatening illness and sickness had been cured like if it was nothing more than a common cold.

We ate like kings while having freedom to move about and explore knowing Auga Naux explored us with open eyes. Maybe we were what they use to be as they look at us like some museum. Every inch of our vessels was explored while in their massive hanger bays. Our President had been giving major medical attention, this along brought her back to fully operation status. Less than a month, she had her command given back placing her in full authority of her once lost Fleet. Three months passed in the blink of an eye.

I was now back in the loop and we have even been given honor for the invasion that took place upon our invaders. We learned that they had been fighting long before we probably even existed and yet neither one was ever conquered. It didn't take long before they dispatched an entire unit to their world. With time our invaders may return to our world but we defeated our enemy but they wasn't completely destroyed.

We can only hope that this is not true knowing they will regain their strength and ability to move about space and time once again. Our conflicts with the Qwzouri has caused them to never return back but we knew they were still out there, maybe even waiting for us. We had this nasty conflict going on between us but for now we were under their protection as we could see them patrolling back and forth. There was so many alien species and somehow they all feared the Auga Naux even though they were among us.

So much we had been told about their world was untrue as they open their arms to us, maybe from us fighting on their side. I guess it was the least they could of have done even though they could've destroyed us for being in their region. There's society seem to be pure from what we could see while and their technology was so highly advance. We had been giving so much, even an escort back home as we learn that we wasn't a secret to this universe, in fact what we had been told from the Universal Commander.

It was true, many aliens have been to our world since our existence but it was only to see the mighty fallen warriors that we once were. We had giving the alien species a choice to return home but only a few chose to stay with us. It was nothing more than understandable now that we have seen the greater picture of what was beyond our so call Dead Solar System, it was our newly name but according to the Universal Protector. We had committed so many violations but at the same time, we have also made so many new friends.

Chapter 25

"Earth"

Once we had return back to our world, it should have been nothing but parades and never ending parties but it was entirely different. Our world was on the verge of destruction from many invaders to our once political system broken in pieces. Our world was almost unlivable in just a short amount of time that we were gone, disease and famine is nearly wiped out our population. It was like we were safer on the Aircraft Carriers, Battleships, Destroyers, our civilization was now equal to know more than vultures preying on each other for mere survival.

We had been welcome in by the Vice President Ayla, so much had happen that there was never another election taking place. Our country had face many invasions, one after another as time continued here on earth for the ones we left behind. It wasn't an easy task from beginning to end, what I was looking at was almost impossible to even visualized, much less imagine. From the looks of what I was seeing, it was hard to believe that we were still the most powerful country in the world but that alone was subject to be question.

We hovered above the ground for several hours before touching down into the oceans as we sat there for several days. I think we were was safer and it wasn't longer after Vice President Ayla had flown aboard. We welcome her but it wasn't until a massive vaccination upon each of us that we might be cleared to return back to land."

"Welcome Vice President Ayla." President Hillary said.

The sight of what I was looking at was truly amazing, it was like if we were in some kind of time capsule. She look as if she had age 30 years although I could be over doing it a little.

"Thank you President Hillary, very happy to be aboard this ship, it looks like if it's been sitting in a salt mine and used for target practice." **Vice President Ayla said.**

"Yes, she has been through a lot over the last few years and we are so happy to see this world again." *President Hillary said.*

It was that moment we were ask to follow them to their briefing room as I watch the Vice President and her Staff takes seats.

"Well, we have been away for more than six years, maybe a little more…we lost contact with time with the many worm holes that took us in world that time seem to not even exist." *"It kind of hard to explain."* **President Hillary said.**

"Madam President, you have been gone a lot longer than that but you look much younger than we expected." *Fleet Admiral Hawick said.*

I could say nothing but remember him as Lt. Jr. Grade before we departed and now this man is holding the rank of Captain. But now that we are back, we will see how long it last because I could tell that President Hilleary wasn't feeling it.

"You are kind of young aren't you for such a prestige rank Fleet Admiral Hawick?" *President Hillary ask.*

"President, you have been gone for a while, and this man has held this rank for the last 3 years and he is doing an excellent job if I may ask." *Vice President Ayla responded.*

"It's understandable Vice President and im not here to question the decision you have made but im back now to assumed duties as Commander in Chief, do you have a problem with it?" *President Hillary ask.*

Silence had come about us as I waited for her to respond as she just sat there looking at her but in so many words. What could she really say about giving up the thrown that she had been holding?

"Vice President, do you have a problem with what I just said." *President Hillary asked loudly.*

"No, when do you want to be sworn back into duty?" *Vice President ask.*

"There is no hurry, so much has happen and I have been going for such a while, few more weeks want hurt anything, give me some time to adjust being back please." *President Hillary ask.*

"Ok, now that we gotten that under control, when are we to be released upon the land? *President Hillary ask.*

"President, you are to remain here until you are all medically cleared due to space virus that you could be carrying." 'Since our many invasion, many Alien Species have brought airborne infection diseases causing death and sickness." Vice President Ayla responded.

"Hello, Madam President, im with (CDC) the World Heath Department, our population is stable but we still face the most common gems." 'Approximately half of our populations is suffering from disease and triples that number in deaths.

"Ok and who are you and why do I need to know this right now?" President Hillary ask.

"Sorry Madam President, im Dr. Struynud and it was me that put your entire Fleet under quarantine for now."

"Please continue." Vice President Ayla ordered him.

The President said nothing back, it was even to my surprising.

"Madam President, virus like Hemorrhagic Ebola fever known as West Nile Virus that is destroying us from contaminant from water to food.

"Vice President, what've you being doing to control this virus?" President Hillary ask.

"President, I have been doing what I can, our funding has not been the same." Vice President Ayla responded.

We all sat for a minute as both of them was giving each other the evil eyes, not one of them blink a wink, it was nothing but amazing…even more so with all that has happen…women…I guess wondering if both of them is bleeding right now.

"I normally don't want to hear your excuses but with all that has happen, this'll not be tolerated from this point on." President responded.

"Madam President, you must understand that this is no one fault, the world health organization estimate that nearly a million cases occur each year and with the population of our Newly Alien Species that've now taking refuge upon our world." 'Disease spreaded by them often cause fever, headaches and skin irritations bringing on confusemeant-poor coordination alone with disturb sleep cycles and neurological damage that often become fatal." Dr. Struynud responded.

"President, the job market that you once known is in jeopardy as we struggle now just to feed our population." 'Our soldiers not just

have to defend what left of us from our world but protect our food supply alone with our farmers." Vice President Ayla responded.

"I'm back now and if we have to come together once again and fight these Aliens form our land, than that just what we must do." President Hillary said.

"President, it may not be as easy as you think it sounds, we were doing exactly just that but with the losing of our soldiers"

"Wait, you tell me all of this but we had some of the best medical facility in the world…producing top doctors!" 'What happen to them?" President Hillary ask.

"President, I was getting to that, all that you talked about did exist but now it's less than a handful, with so many invasions upon us." 'Each one brought a different type of destructions and our gold supply is down to nothing, most of it was taken from this world." Vice President Ayla explained.

"You mean they stole it?" President Hillary said loudly.

"No, it was taken, we fought hard to protect our gold reserve but with the deaths of our soldiers that gave all they had, it was taking." Vice President Ayla said calmly.

"You sit so none- shalaunt about this like if it is nothing!" President Hillary-Hilary said.

"You need to calm down President, there is no need for your loud tone of voice here, im giving you a breakdown of all that has happen." And you will respect me while im still in power, now do we have and understanding President Hillary?" Vice President Ayla ask aggressively.

"My apology Vice President, so much has happen and I have been gone so long. We now need to take this one phase at a time until we are back on track." President Hillary said.

Everyone had gotten quiet but it was understandable, we had two women here, one went to fight and invading force, while the other stayed behind keeping America together.

"President, I have been doing my best to keep the peace with these Alien Species that has taking haven upon our land and now I suggest when you take command, that you do the same." Vice President Ayla ask.

"Do you have contact with these Alien Invaders?" President Hillary ask mildly.

"President, with all that has happen."

"You don't!" President Hillary ask.

"No and they are known to move around without notice with the seasons and unknown weather conditions. Vice President Ayla said.

"I want to know about these diseases that we are facing." President Hillary ask.

"So many we are up against like cholera that births in Indian subcontinent and Russia and sub Saharan Africa causing death by dehydration and it an acute infection of the intestine and severe diarrhea." Dr. Struynud said.

"How is this possible if it exist in other places as well?" President Hillary ask.

"Madam President, with so much world travel now, these unknowns move among us now almost overnight but cryptosporidiosis is the most common from waterborne disease and it also found throughout the rest of the world.

"I never heard of this, how're we affected?" President Hillary ask.

"Parasite bringing on stomach pains similar to Rotavirus in which causes viral gastroenteritis worldwide or Typhoid that causes over 600.000 yearly." 'Or, Yellow fever that estimates 30.000 annual deaths or bleeding from the mouth, nose, eyes and even deterioration of the kidneys." Dr. Struynud said.

"That enough for now Dr." Vice President said.

"I would like to hear more Dr, if you don't mind." President Hillary ask.

This was nothing more than a display of power between the ruler and the one soon to be out of office.

"We have new virus among us now like Dengue Fever from the Aegyptus mosquito from Asia and Africa causing hemorrhaging circulatory failure similar to Malaria or Pneumonia that usually infection of the streptococcus or mycoplasma, its bacteria can live in the human without notice for years." Dr. Struynud explained.

"Is that it?" President Hillary ask.

"No, we are living in a world of diseases like Japanese Encephalitis in which is a mosquito borne disease endemic or Onchocerciasis spawn in Africa that causes visual impairment, rashes, lesions, intense itching, skin depigmentation and lymphadenitis." 'Hepatitis A, B, C, Influenza, Meningitis, Tuberculosis and not to mention that our

soil is be infested with a new fungal alone with our plants and trees."
'This alone is known to be were ever the aliens have occupied most is
harmful to our health." Dr. Struynud explained.

He told us how he could go on but the Vice President had brought it
to an end.

"With so much destroying us from what in, what can we do to
bring this to an end?" President Hilary ask.

"We are doing all we can but with limited resources, these infection can
be very challenging as we lack laboratories and infrastructure but it's not just
with us." This is happening all around the world." Vice President Ayla said.

"If I may add Madam President, the way we are dying, the human
race will end within 100 years easily and this planet will belong to
our Alien Invaders." 'You may not know but the sound of children's
laughter is rare, our women aren't bearing life anymore." 'But maybe
it's the radiation from explosions of our own nuclear weapons done by
the aliens themselves. "Dr. Struynud responded.

"You are telling me that, our world is filled with radiation?" President
Hillary ask.

"That is correct, our world is contaminated with radiation, we are
basically defenseless...many of our own nuke exploded within their
own silos. Vice president explained.

"How many countries?" President Hillary ask.

"Worldwide mostly." Vice President Ayla responded.

"How did this happen and when?" President ask.

"They were our Antillean Invaders and it's been about 13 years
now as we are rebuilding, the ground shielded us. But it didn't stop it
entirely, our earth is now polluted, but other Alien Species have come
and cleaned up our earth little by little." 'We have now become an
open gate way for any and all to come." Vice President Ayla responded.

There really wasn't no need to go any farther, we did destroy their
worlds but during the war knowing from what we just heard. We have lost
complete control and this is our outcome, they navigated their way back
to ours world doing the same to us.

"Does Area51 still exist?" President Hillary ask.

"No, it was raided and destroyed and that entire area is occupied by the
Gyuonei Species." Vice President Ayla said.

"The desert, there is nothing out there but dirt." President Hillary said.

"Not anymore, there an entire alien species and they are very territorial alone with many others species that has occupied our land." Vice President Ayla explained.

"How can this be?" President Hillary ask.

"When you are cleared to enter, there are ISUP's that have been hovering over us but they have been a big help as well." Vice President Ayla said.

"Yes, we encountered them several days back as reentered our galaxy, they are not far from us now." President Hillary said.

Several months passed and the President had been given control of the White House, nothing about this had become easy on a daily basis. Our military was barely able to function and we seem to be getting back on track. I have been offered to be re-commissioned but it was better that I turned it down and find some peace in the remainder of my life. We had been gone more than 10 years and it showed, maybe it was all the strange food we have been given.

But we all felt stronger than the average human knowing now, none of us should take nothing for granted. Not even this beef that we had been serve, it was nothing more than a treat because livestock was now highly protected. This world that we once defended with our very lives before we left was now under massive invasion of many alien species. We now suffered from many unknown airborne virus causing infections. Our own military alone with law enforcement type agencies is now force to kill Americans, some had become nothing more than living zombies. It was Christmas day and from this moment on, it will never be the same as we known it. We had come so close to none existence.

If it wasn't for the technology and help from another Alien Life Form we would have been completely wipe off from the face of this earth. They gave us the technology of defying gravity alone with weapons that brought on our Invaders destruction. They taught us how to recalibrate our weapons making them hundred times more dangerous. Time itself will be decided on what is to happen to humanity worldwide now. For our lives will never be the same from this Earth Invasion.

Printed in the United States
By Bookmasters